Thumbprint Mysteries

GORY ALLELUIA

BY

MARY BLOUNT CHRISTIAN

CB

CONTEMPORARY BOOKS

a division of NTC/CONTEMPORARY PUBLISHING GROUP
Lincolnwood, Illinois USA

Thumbprint
Mysteries

MORE THUMBPRINT MYSTERIES

by Mary Blount Christian:

Fatal Fiction
Murder on the Menu

This is a work of fiction. The characters, incidents, and dialogues are products of the author's imagination and are not to be construed as real. Any resemblance to actual events or persons, living or dead, is entirely coincidental.

Cover Illustration: Larry Didona

ISBN: 0-8092-0674-9

Published by Contemporary Books,
a division of NTC/Contemporary Publishing Group, Inc.,
4255 West Touhy Avenue,
Lincolnwood (Chicago), Illinois 60646-1975 U.S.A.
© 1998 Mary Blount Christian

890 QB 0 9 8 7 6 5 4 3 2 1

CHAPTER 1

Lin Mendoza Hill settled into her swivel chair and flipped the page on her desk calendar—May 5th. She smiled, remembering *Cinco de Mayo* from her youth. As a daughter of migrant farmworkers in rural Texas, she recalled that it was a time of celebration of Mexican independence, *la fiesta de la patria*.

It did not matter how hard the day in the fields was. It did not matter how aching the muscles were. Men, women, and children celebrated. They dressed in inherited costumes worn for only the most special occasions. The *mariachis*, the musicians, pulled out their scarred guitars and dented trumpets. They played and danced, and life was good. They celebrated Mexico's independence and their ancestors who won it. It didn't matter if they were citizens of the United States. It didn't matter if they came with a visa or slipped across the river at night. Everyone celebrated.

The farm owners came to watch. They convinced themselves that the workers were happy and satisfied. But how could anyone be satisfied being old and worn-out at 50? How could one be happy, traveling from farm to farm, following the crops, with no place on earth that was truly their own ground? The celebration made them forget for the moment. But the reality and its headaches were all there the next morning at dawn.

Her father, Guillermo Mendoza, took satisfaction that his family could out-pick any other family. Strawberries or cotton, beans or grapefruit, it did not matter to them. He took happiness that they were all together. He was so sure that his children would get away from the dreary, nomadic life.

"The United States will reward you with good jobs and much happiness," he told his children, gathered about his feet. Then he would laugh and tell them how he came to Texas—twice. "I was 14 the first time, and I was too small to cross the Rio Bravo alone."

"Rio Grande, Papa," Lin would interrupt.

Papa would smile. "*Sí*, on this side of the river, it is *Río Grande*, Big River. But on the other side, it is *Río Bravo*, Brave River. A few Mexicans had saved enough *pisto* to pay a guide to carry them on his shoulders. That way they did not arrive wet. The border guards—they looked for Mexicans with wet clothes. It meant they had just crossed the river. So I bundled my clothes on top of my head and carefully stepped into the river where those ahead of me stepped, as that would be the shallowest water. On the American side, I quickly slipped into my shirt and pants, and I ran as the dim light of flashlights bounced along the bank toward me. I hid in a train boxcar. I thought I was being very smart! The train can carry me deep into Texas, I thought."

Then Papa would laugh. "Imagine my surprise when I awakened the next day and found myself right back in Mexico! I had hidden in a southbound train, and it took me home. I decided that was a sign that I should wait until I could get a legal visa. I am glad, because it was at the immigration office that I met your mama, *mi tesora*, my treasure."

Lin and her siblings listened many times to Papa's story, and they never grew tired of it. They never tired of dreaming with Papa of the good things that America would give to them. Lin sighed wistfully. Dreams do not always come true. Several siblings lay in infant graves in the pauper cemeteries. Her younger sister Carmelita married a migrant at 16 and died in childbirth. Guillermo, Jr., moved to California where he joined the migrant movement working for better conditions. Only Lin, Belinda Esperanza Mendoza, left the fields on an academic scholarship. She left most of her name there. She became simply Lin Mendoza, then Lin Hill, using the surname of her short-lived marriage. Only she left rural Texas for New York City and a job as an editor at Indeco Publishing. Lin crossed her arms and hugged herself sighing. *Ah, la vida en la ciudad grande*; life in the big city. She missed her family.

Lin had an idea. She buzzed the intercom. "Bess, do I have any appointments after lunch?" She toyed with the onyx and polished brass trophy as she spoke. It was a reward from Indeco for editing the most profitable books last year, and just the right size for restless hands to tinker with.

"No, you're free. You leaving early?" Bess said. "Oh, by the way, *saludos*, or whatever the proper word is."

"You remembered. *Gracias*." Lin wanted to prepare *carne asada, chiles rellenos, quesadillas,* and *flan* for an early supper. What fiesta was complete without grilled beef strips, stuffed peppers, cheese on tortillas, and vanilla pudding? No matter how much she wanted to forget the hardships, she clung to them as she clung to the warmth of her family. They were all part of who she was: resilient but determined. "I don't want Jeffrey to forget my half of his heritage," she added.

"Good idea," Bess said. "I won't let anyone hold you here, just in case someone gets a bright idea."

"Thanks. And would you try ringing Delia again, please?"

Lin bit her lip. It was not like Delia Dorrs to be late on a manuscript. Delia was secretive; that was part of her contract. The fewer people who knew the contents, the fewer leaks reached the public. Secrecy guaranteed a peak of interest when the book hit the stores. Delia wrote exposé nonfiction.

Her books had brought down senators and heads of major corporations. Sports heroes and entertainment stars lost revenue after her biting accounts of their secret lives. She turned over rocks and exposed unknown problems to the public. It made her the most sought-after author for interviews. It also made her one of the most hated by the wealthy and influential. One talk-show host said, "She kisses princes and turns them into frogs."

Delia delighted in the threats she got and in the many lawsuits. Indeco took out extra insurance against libel because of Delia. Most suits were dropped. What could the subjects do? She was accurate, completely accurate. Everything she wrote was well documented, much of it in public records that no one else had bothered to dig out. Truth was the best defense, and Delia dealt in the truth, no matter how dirty it was.

Bess came into the office with a stack of large brown envelopes. The flow of manuscripts never stopped. "Still no answer at Delia's," Bess said. "Want me to keep trying?"

Lin tapped the desk with her pencil, biting her lip in thought. "She or her secretary should be there; I don't understand. Tell you what: keep trying, and if you reach her, at least find out what the title is. Marketing needs something to promote."

Marketing hated being kept in the dark; so did she, for that matter. "Give me a call tonight if you will, Bess. I'm taking Jeffrey on an outing tomorrow. Maybe we'll just make it an all-day trip in the Connecticut countryside; I want to look through some of those antique shops anyway. I'll drop by Delia's and leave her a note if she's not there. Perhaps I can light a fire under her to get that manuscript in."

Bess laughed. "Antique shopping? Oh, I'm sure Jeffrey will just love that! Wouldn't any eight-year-old boy?"

Lin tossed her pencil onto her desk. She laughed. "I know, but we'll also stop off for lunch at the Swan Inn. He loves watching the swans and the waterfalls. And we'll find other things to do. We just need to get on the road a bit; I haven't had a chance yet to try out my new car."

New car? It was a vintage Volkswagen Beetle that was sorely in need of a paint job and body specialist. Although basically dark blue, it had a green door and a red fender, probably gathered from junkyards. The motor sounded like an old lawnmower. But it was her special find in the classifieds, and she was delighted to have her own wheels. It was just right for day trips.

She had time to grocery shop before Jeffrey got home. The eye-watering odor of jalapeño peppers filled the little car. But what was a *Cinco de Mayo* meal without the main ingredient? She felt only a small pang of guilt that she bought ready-made tortillas. At home, she chopped the onion, tomatoes, garlic, green and red peppers, and the jalapeños. She wanted plenty of *pico de gallo* to go with the sour cream, guacamole, and quesadillas.

While the meat mixture simmered on the range, Lin went into the bedroom. She found the colorful circular skirt in the back of her closet. Lace-trimmed tiers of red, gold, green, and white were gathered and ruffled to swing with every movement. She held it to her and swayed in front of the full-length mirror. Lin smiled. Closing her eyes, she imagined the music playing.

She could almost hear the bystanders clapping and shouting, "Yi, yi, ieeeeeee." She could almost see the younger ones whirling faster and faster until they fell into the dust, exhausted and laughing.

Lin dressed in her embroidered peasant blouse and the skirt. She pulled her dark hair back over one ear so that the gold hoop earring showed. Then she called her former in-laws, who lived next door in the duplex, and invited them over for an authentic *Cinco de Mayo* fiesta.

When Jeffrey got home, she had him change into a white shirt and dark pants. She tied a red bandanna at his neck. "If only I had a *serape* for you," she said. "You would wear it over one shoulder and the two of us would whirl and stomp our feet until the music stopped."

"Lin, you miss Texas, don't you?" Mrs. Hill said at dinner.

"The heat, the humidity, the earthy smells, the friends—yes, I miss. The life, no," Lin said sadly. "That I never want to see again."

Mr. Hill pushed back from the table and patted his stomach. "I don't think my tongue will ever taste again," he said, laughing, "but I did enjoy the feast, Lin. Thanks for sharing this."

After they left, Lin loaded the dishwasher and set it running. She scooted Jeffrey off for his bath and bedtime. Flopping on the couch, she pulled out Papa's battered old guitar and tried unsuccessfully to pick out a song from her past. Maybe someday she would take lessons, she thought. Or perhaps Jeffrey would.

The phone rang. It was Bess. "I tried all afternoon, Lin. I even called just now from home. There is no answer at Delia's."

Lin thanked her for trying. "I'll stop by there tomorrow."

The next morning she got Jeffrey out of bed and fed him *huevos rancheros*—an omelet made with salsa. "For lunch, it's anything you want at the Swan Inn," she promised. "I don't want to burn out your stomach lining with all these *tejano* specialties." She tousled his hair, laughing.

Lin borrowed the cellular phone from the Hills, since this was the first time to take her new Beetle on the road. She put a small ice chest with bottled water and fruit in the trunk.

Because they got a late start, Lin skipped the antique shops—to Jeffrey's delight, she imagined. Instead she stopped at the Swan Inn where they ate on the little enclosed porch with the waterfalls and swan activity in full view of their window-side table. After last night's red-hot menu, Lin ordered baked fish and a potato.

From there she drove the twisting, narrow road to the heavily wooded estate of Delia Dorrs. The high iron spike fence seemed out of place in this area where carefully piled stones formed property boundaries, but Delia had reason to be cautious. She had made many enemies. The double gate across the drive displayed twin brass D's. Lin smiled. Delia was cautious but still brazen.

The gates were locked. A camera was aimed directly where any car would park. There was an intercom on a post at car-window height. Lin pushed the "talk" button and waited. There was no answer. Through the dense brush that bordered the fence and drive, she could see a tiny bit of red. That must be Delia's Porsche. Lin rang again. When there was still no answer, she grabbed the cell phone and dialed. She could hear the ring from here. Delia had a pool out back, and she had an outdoor ringer for her phone. Lin honked the horn impatiently. "This is ridiculous," Lin said. "What's going on here?"

A movement on the drive, low to the ground, caught her attention. Lin got out of the car and walked toward the gate. Peering through the bars she saw a massive palomino-colored dog—a Great Dane. Lin recognized the dog from when she visited here once. "Sweetpea?" she called. The dog whimpered and rolled over, belly up.

Dark stains covered his legs and side. "Come here, boy. What's the matter?" Lin called. She shook the gate. The lock held. Remembering Delia's instructions about introducing oneself to a dog, Lin pushed her hand through the bars and held it palm up, indicating that she meant Sweetpea no harm.

Sweetpea belly-crawled to the gate and sniffed her hand. Hesitantly, Lin touched Sweetpea's leg. She jerked her hand back from the sticky substance that covered one side of the dog. Lin stared at her hand. Blood? That poor dog was hurt badly, judging from all the blood. Delia would be terribly upset if anything happened to Sweetpea.

Lin hated the sight of blood. Nausea overwhelmed her, and she grabbed the gate to steady herself. Lin took deep breaths. *Get hold of yourself*, she chided. Glancing back at the car, she said, "Jeffrey, stay in the car. I'm going to climb over the fence. I think Sweetpea is hurt."

Gingerly, Lin searched for toeholds in the gate as she made her way up and over the top. Cautiously, she dropped to the ground. Instead of lying there to be coddled and examined, Sweetpea immediately leaped up. He trotted toward the house; he didn't move now as if he were hurt.

He stopped and turned toward Lin, barking that deep baritone bark. He could be intimidating to anyone who didn't know his name was Sweetpea. It became obvious to Lin that he wanted her to follow him. She hesitated as a cold chill crept up her spine. She could feel the hairs on the back of her neck stand up. A terrible feeling engulfed Lin like a chilled night mist. Something was wrong. She called back to Jeffrey. "Watch the clock on the dash. If I am not back in five minutes, dial *9, and tell whoever answers to get to Ms. Dorrs's house as quickly as possible. Lock the doors and stay inside. You understand?"

Satisfied that Jeffrey understood, she said, "Okay, Sweetpea, show me."

He trotted a few feet, then waited. When Lin followed, he trotted and waited. He led her to the back of the house. There Lin saw that the patio was covered with his bloody footprints, yet he didn't limp. The sliding glass door was ajar wide enough for him to slip through. "Delia!" Lin yelled. She cupped her hands to the glass and peered inside.

Pictures hung crooked on the walls, furniture was toppled, and books lay scattered over the floor. And lying face up, eyes staring directly at Lin but unseeing, was Delia. Blood glistened on her head like rubies and formed a wide, dark stain on the thick white carpet.

Lin felt her face go numb. Her body felt like rubber. She clutched at the door handle to keep from falling. Everything faded as if in a black-and-white movie, then went blank.

CHAPTER 2

Clutching the door handle was the last thing that Lin remembered until she was vaguely aware of someone's strong arms wrapped around her, lifting her to a sitting position. She moaned groggily, "Hmmmm." It was nice to be held so gently, to feel so safe. Someone was calling her name. She smiled, not wanting to wake from the dream.

The euphoria suddenly lifted like a window shade snapping. Her eyes popped open, and she was staring into the clear blue eyes of a stranger.

The fog vanished, and she remembered Delia lying in a pool of blood. Jeffrey! She had left Jeffrey in the car. "Jeffrey!" She clutched the lapels of the stranger's pale blue jumpsuit. "My son! Where is Jeffrey?"

"He's all right, Mrs. Hill. He's playing with that monster of a dog under the watchful eyes of Officer Wingate," the man said. "Take it easy. Don't try to get up just yet. You've got a small but nasty gash and bump on your head."

Lin tried to focus her eyes on the name tag above the man's shirt pocket. STATE OF CONNECTICUT; OFFICE OF THE MEDICAL EXAMINER. Coroner? "Jeffrey didn't—didn't—"

"Your son didn't see any of this. He did exactly what you told him. He said he watched the dash clock and then called *9 on the cellular phone. He's a good kid." He smiled at her, showing two rows of perfectly straight, gleaming white teeth.

As he spoke, Lin studied his face. She didn't meet such gorgeous men in real life. And if he wasn't real, then neither was Delia, lying there, staring out with a look of shock on her face. Lin told herself that perhaps she was just in a dream. Yes, the nightmare had turned into a nice, pleasant dream.

Lin stared at the lapels where she had clutched the stranger's—the medical examiner's—jumpsuit. Dark red stains. Trembling, she pulled her hands up and stared at them as if they belonged to someone else. An icy chill crept up her backbone. Bile rose in her throat. "I'm going to be sick," she said.

The man handed her a large bag. "Have at it," he said. "It's okay."

When she had relieved herself of that expensive fish from Swan Inn, he placed his hand on the back of her neck and gently pushed her head forward. "Just sit here with your head between your knees a few minutes." He paused. "Would you like for me to call your husband to come for your son?"

"No!" Lin said. "That is, I'm divorced. I could call his grandparents in Queens, but by the time they got here, we would be free to leave anyway, right? Uh, sorry about your shoes. Guess my aim is pretty bad."

He smiled sympathetically. "All in a day's work."

She shook her head sadly. "Poor Delia. How horrible." She closed her eyes, trying to block out the sight of those staring eyes. Why didn't they cover her?

A second voice startled her. "What happened, Mrs. Hill? Was there a struggle? Was it self-defense?"

Lin blinked at the second man, a broad figure dressed in a state police uniform. "Ms. Hill," she corrected. "How would I know? Oh, surely you don't think—"

"Let her get her bearings, Trey," the medical examiner said. "She has a bad bump and cut on her head, probably when she fainted. She could have a mild concussion, and that will cloud her thoughts for a while. She ought to be x-rayed." Even as he spoke to the officer, he didn't take his eyes off Lin.

Lin shifted uncomfortably under his direct and intense gaze. Maybe it wasn't his clear blue eyes that intrigued her, although that would certainly be enough. When he looked at her, it was as if she were the only other person there.

The one called Trey said, "Or she could have got it in the struggle."

"Delia was dead when I got here!" Lin said. "I followed Sweetpea—"

"Sweetpea?" Trey interrupted.

"The dog. He looked as if he were hurt. He was really stressed out and wanted me to follow him." She stared at her hands. "This is Delia's blood, not Sweetpea's?" She would have thrown up again if she could, but she had nothing left. "You know my name. But who are you?"

"Sorry, Ms. Hill," the one in the blue jumpsuit said. "I'm Craig Gleason from the Office of the Chief Medical Examiner. And this is Lieutenant Perry Trey of the Statewide Cooperative Crime Control Task Force."

Flashes of light inside the house caught Lin's attention. A photographer was taking photos of the crime scene. She whimpered. "I—I want to see Jeffrey. I want to see my son."

"Not just yet," Lieutenant Trey said.

"For heaven's sake, Trey," Dr. Gleason said. "I'll take responsibility to see that she doesn't run off." He reached down and pulled Lin up with no effort. Lin was five feet, five inches, tall for a *tejano*. He was a good ten inches taller and broad of shoulder. She smiled her gratitude. That determined jawline told Lin a lot about him. It went well with those clear, steadily probing blue eyes and slightly pouty lips. *What a beautiful character for a book*, she thought. *He'd wow the women readers.* She told herself that she was probably thinking about him to keep from thinking about Delia. Disassociation? Denial? Lin felt her legs wobble; she was weaker than she had realized.

Dr. Gleason took her hand and wrapped one arm about her shoulders to steady her. "Before you see Jeffrey, I need to take samples of the blood on your hands and from your head wound. Don't be alarmed, Ms. Hill," he said, leading her to a folding patio chair. His voice was soft and assuring. "This is just routine."

Lin searched his handsome face for a sign of suspicion. "That's what they say in the cop shows just before they slap the cuffs on," she said.

He grinned at her. There was a mischievous glint in his eyes although Lin could see nothing funny about the situation. "That's because they are guilty, Ms. Hill. Incidentally, that's Craig Gleason, M.D. So I am serious when I recommend that you get your head x-rayed."

"I should have it examined for coming out here in the first place," she muttered.

He grinned at her and shook his head. Putting on a fresh

set of latex gloves, he swabbed the blood on her hands. He placed the swabs into evidence bags and labeled them in bold letters. On a clipboard, he drew diagrams of a right and a left hand and marked where he'd taken each sample.

Another man dressed much like Trey strolled by. "How are things at the morgue, Doc?"

"Pretty dead, Roy," Dr. Gleason said.

The officer trotted off, chuckling to himself.

Dr. Gleason glanced up at Lin, frowning slightly. "Sorry about that, Ms. Hill. We couldn't live with ourselves if we didn't project a little dark humor now and then." He smiled at her and her revulsion melted.

Replacing his gloves with fresh ones, Dr. Gleason swabbed her cut, speaking quietly as he did. "Don't worry about this, Ms. Hill. This is merely to eliminate your blood sample from that of the victim's and perhaps the murderer's if he or she also lost blood in the struggle. Where are you staying tonight, Ms. Hill?"

Lin felt like a curious bystander and not a participant in the proceedings. "Home, in Queens. Why?"

"I asked because I'm concerned about your head, Ms. Hill. If you plan on driving back to Queens, then you will definitely have to have an x-ray before I can allow you on the road. You wouldn't want to pass out and have a wreck now, would you?"

"Of course not!" Lin said. Her head did feel twice its normal size. Everything looked slightly out of focus too. Maybe he had a point. She wouldn't want to endanger Jeffrey just to show her independence.

He placed the bagged samples into the small chest he carried. "Now," he said. "Let's get the blood off you so that you can go see your son." He used alcohol swabs and gently wiped her hands. She felt as if she were a child again, and she couldn't resist staring at his face. He seemed unaware of his good looks. And he was gentle and thoughtful. What a nice combination. The only downside, besides that he was no doubt married, was that his work called for dead bodies. Lin shuddered involuntarily.

He glanced up, concern etched across his face. "You feeling okay?"

"Yeah." She blushed, just glad he was an M.E. and not a mind reader. How could she even be thinking about him? So that she would not have to think about Delia? At least she hoped that was the only reason. Crushes were for teens. "I'm okay. I just want to see Jeffrey."

He took Lin by the arm and called back over his shoulder. "I'm taking this lady to see her son, Trey. I promise I shall return your *witness*." He put special emphasis on the word *witness*.

They walked down the gravel drive toward the gate. He had not let go of her arm. Was he concerned that she'd fall, or that she might bolt and run? Not that she objected. To the contrary. Lin suddenly stopped. "Do I look all right?"

He grinned. "You look great." He looked down at his feet, and Lin could almost believe he was embarrassed. "I mean, yeah, no signs of trauma to scare your son. The bump I'm concerned about is at your hairline, so it won't alarm him. There won't be a scar, once it's back to normal."

"Thanks," Lin said, grinning slightly, "for both reassurances."

As they rounded the last stand of underbrush, Lin saw Jeffrey and Sweetpea having a tug-of-war with a stick. Someone had cleaned the blood off the dog. Officer Wingate—Officer Angela Wingate, as it turned out— leaned against Lin's Volkswagen, watching. She straightened up as they approached.

"Mom, Mom, he likes me. Watch this!" Jeffrey shouted. He threw the stick, and Sweetpea took two galloping strides and returned with the stick, shoving it at Jeffrey. "Mom, are they going to arrest Sweetpea? Don't let them, Mom!"

"Arrest?" Lin said, clutching Jeffrey to her. He smelled of earthy sweat and dog slobber. She looked at Officer Wingate and raised one brow in question.

"Yes, ma'am," Officer Wingate said. "That is, the subject will be impounded until the authorities determine proper disposal."

"Disposal!" Lin gasped.

"Wingate," Dr. Gleason said, "choose your words with caution, for heaven's sake." He turned those beautiful blue eyes back to Lin. "What she should have said is that he will be impounded, and if there is no arrangement in the will, the pound will keep him for an appointed time. However, if no one claims him or offers to purchase him for the cost of the upkeep, then . . ."

Lin finished the sentence for him. "Disposal." She looked at Jeffrey and Sweetpea bouncing around in the dirt, wrestling and having a great time together. "Sweetpea is a witness to the murder," Lin said. "Do you go about destroying witnesses?"

Dr. Gleason laughed. "A witness? A dog? Seriously, I will not let Sweetpea come to a violent end, I promise, even if I have to take him in myself." He cocked his head toward Jeffrey and Sweetpea. "However, I live alone, and he wouldn't be as happy with me as with—" He nodded toward Jeffrey.

The point that he lived alone was not lost on Lin, but she concentrated on the main theme: Sweetpea. "You're not serious!" Lin said. "I live in a little duplex in Queens with Jeffrey and a jealous, obsessive, and, I might add, vindictive cat. Look at my little car! And you want me to take in this canine Godzilla?" She sighed. Jeffrey was having a blast, and Sweetpea was no longer the whimpering coward that she first came upon. "All right, but strictly on a trial basis," she insisted. "I'm not promising anything permanent. Besides which, Lieutenant Trey seems intent on locking me away."

"He doesn't get much excitement in his job out here among the rich and famous," Dr. Gleason said. "Cut him some slack. He'll come back to reality soon. Now let's get back so you can answer a few questions, okay?" He turned toward Officer Wingate. "I have some orange juice and soft drinks in the red chest in my van. Why don't you and Jeffrey serve yourselves. We'll be back in a few minutes."

Lin liked his confidence. And she liked that he was still holding her arm to steady her. Not that she wasn't steady enough on her own by now. Especially after seeing that Jeffrey was all right. But it was nice being looked after for a little while. She was as '90s a woman as any, but she yearned for companionship, even a little coddling and cradling now and again.

Several men in jumpsuits like Dr. Gleason's milled about the patio and inside the house with small brushes, swabs, and notebooks. They had covered Delia's body with a white tarp. Yet Lin knew exactly what she looked like under that tarp; it was an image she would carry forever. Dr. Gleason ushered Lin to a folding patio chair by the pool. He pulled his own chair closeby. Grasping her wrist between his thumb and fingers, he checked her pulse, frowning slightly. Next he took her blood pressure.

Lieutenant Trey scraped a chair along the stone walk and set it to face Lin. He frowned at Dr. Gleason.

"I'll stay. Something she says could speed along my conclusions," the doctor said. "Besides, her pulse is too high, as is her blood pressure. Also I'm concerned about that head injury."

Trey shrugged. "Okay, from the top, Mrs.—Ms. Hill. How did you know Miss Dorrs and why were you here?"

Lin explained that she was an editor at Indeco Publishing and Delia was her author. "When I couldn't reach her all day yesterday and into the night, I decided to check for myself during our trip—that is, Jeffrey's and mine. When I saw blood all over Sweetpea, I climbed the fence to see, and that's when he led me to—to Delia's body. I guess I passed out."

Lieutenant Trey wrote in his notebook a moment, then looked up at Lin. "You say you tried all yesterday to contact her?"

"Yes, now I know why."

Lieutenant Trey was staring at her through narrow eye slits. "Ms. Hill, you say the victim was probably dead yesterday because you didn't get through to her on the telephone. But you see from the condition of the body, she is only recently deceased. I believe that when Dr. Gleason here does his full autopsy, he'll find that Miss Dorrs did not die yesterday. Instead, she died today, so it could have been you who murdered her."

CHAPTER
3

Lin clutched the metal arms of the chair. "That's ridiculous! I had no reason to kill Delia. And if I did, would I bring my little boy along? That's sick! *You're* sick to even think such a thing."

"That is just what I'd expect a murderer to do," Lieutenant Trey said. His tone was irritatingly low-key. "It would take away suspicion."

"Well, it certainly didn't take away yours, did it?" She turned to Dr. Gleason. "How did this man get his badge? Through the mail?"

Dr. Gleason netted his thick dark brows into a frown—a warning, Lin assumed, that she shouldn't antagonize the man. Lin leaned back and clutched her head. "Can I have an aspirin, please? My head hurts something awful."

"I am concerned that Ms. Hill may have a concussion," Dr. Gleason told Trey. "As a physician, I insist that you cut this interview short until I've had a chance to x-ray her."

Trey mumbled under his breath and closed his notepad. "Don't leave the state," he said.

"I live in New York," Lin persisted. She pulled a business card from her purse. "This is my work number and address. And I'm jotting my home address and phone number on the back. I am not going anywhere but there. Please, just let me get my son home and away from this."

"I insist," Dr. Gleason said. "You don't want to be sued later for not allowing proper medical attention. I'd testify truthfully that I recommended x-rays immediately."

Lieutenant Trey grabbed the card. "I am holding you completely responsible, understand?" At last, a bit of inflection in his voice, Lin noticed.

Dr. Gleason gave his men the okay to bag and remove Delia's body onto a gurney and wheel it outside.

"Thank you for your help, but please, let me get my son out of here before they take her through the gate," Lin begged.

Dr. Gleason held up his hand. "Wait," he called to his men. He went over to them and spoke in quiet tones. He returned to get Lin. "It's okay. They'll wait. For now, I want to take you in for an x-ray." He peeled off the jumpsuit he'd worn over his regular clothes.

He was wearing a blue denim shirt and well-fitted jeans, Lin noticed. Did he choose his clothes for comfort or to go with his eyes, she wondered. She pulled back. "At the morgue?"

Dr. Gleason grinned. "We prefer to call it a lab, but no, at a private clinic. It's all right. I promise."

Reluctantly, Lin walked toward the gate. "My car," Lin insisted. "I am not riding in anything that has coroner or medical examiner, whatever, written on the side."

"I drive," Dr. Gleason said. "You are not getting behind

the wheel until I believe it is safe."

He arranged for one of his men to drive his van back to the lab in Farmington and stow the evidence and Delia's body in the cool, sterile lockers. He motioned to Jeffrey and Sweetpea to get into the back of the Volkswagen. When he had helped Lin into the passenger side, he slid behind the wheel.

The private clinic was a small, one-story building of stone and mortar on the main road about three miles from Delia's estate. "I am part owner of this little clinic, although I rarely make use of it," he said, smiling that perfect smile at her. Dr. Gleason stopped the car in front and hurried around to the passenger side to help Lin. "Sorry, Jeffrey, but I'm afraid I can't let Sweetpea inside the clinic. Why don't you two go into the backyard? There are plastic tunnels and slides and plenty to play with." He turned to Lin. "It solves lots of problems when patients bring kids along."

He took the x-rays and disappeared into the room next to the radiology room. He returned with a pain reliever and water. "I was right, Lin—is that all right to call you Lin? You do have a slight concussion. You should be all right in a few days with proper rest, but I cannot let you get behind the wheel tonight. It isn't safe."

"I'm going home, Craig," Lin said emphatically. She made a point to call him by his first name since he had used hers. Lin had dealt with professional men before, especially doctors, who create a chain of command by calling her by her first name. Usually they were taken aback when she called them by their given names; they usually switched back to the more formal attitude. She didn't get that feeling from this man, though. He seemed comfortable with it. "Jeffrey needs to be home. I need to be home. This has been a horrible experience. I badly need to be surrounded by the familiar."

"Then I'll drive you," Craig said. He measured out a length of gauze and cut it from the spool.

"But then you'd be in Queens." As intriguing as that sounded to Lin, that was definitely not in the plans.

His eyes twinkled in the florescent light, and his expression was one of bemusement. "I wasn't suggesting anything improper, Lin." He folded the gauze into a soft pad and swabbed her head wound as he spoke.

"Sorry, I didn't mean to imply that you did," Lin said. She wanted to trust people again, but it was difficult.

"I'll just hook a tow to your Beetle and attach my motor," Craig explained. He picked up a bottle and several swabs. "I'm using surgical glue so that stitches won't be necessary."

"Motor?" she repeated.

"My Harley. You don't think I go around all the time in my M.E. wagon, do you?"

"I guess I hadn't given it a lot of thought," Lin said, even though she had. She had imagined him pulling up in front on a date. She could imagine the rush of curious neighbors coming to see who had died and the helpful ones with their casseroles and freshly baked breads.

"I'll be back at the lab by morning and can start on the victim," he said. "There, all done."

Lin shuddered. She didn't like the idea of anyone *starting on* Delia. "Her name is Delia—Delia Dorrs."

He smiled tolerantly. "We learn to forget that, Lin. It's not as hard to do an autopsy on a number as it is on a name. Is there anyone else who can look after you and wake you every few hours to be sure you are all right?"

"Else?" she echoed. Did he mean Jeffrey or himself? "Yes, my ex-in-laws live next door. But is that necessary?"

"Yes, it is definitely necessary. I don't want you slipping into a coma." Craig made a slight face. "That must be awkward, I mean, beginning a new relationship with your ex's parents next door."

Lin smiled. "Probably no more difficult than you with your coroner's—er, medical examiner's—wagon. No, they're great. They take care of Jeffrey after school instead of having him in day care, and they actually encourage me to look for someone special."

"And have you found anyone?" he asked casually as he replaced the surgical glue and gauze into the cabinet. He had his head turned so that she could not see his expression this time.

"No," she replied. "But it's not their fault. Mom keeps bringing home guys to introduce to me." She sighed. "You know the old saying about once burned. I wouldn't object if the right guy showed up someday, but until then, I enjoy my own company and I'm fine just as it is." He was looking at her again as if he knew that she was lying. Lin squirmed uneasily under the steady gaze of those clear blue eyes. *Shut up, Lin. You're talking too much. Is it the concussion, or does this man have you babbling so?*

Craig prepared the car for the tow and hooked his motorcycle securely. He called Jeffrey and Sweetpea and everyone piled into the cramped car. Craig started the car and said, "I think we'd better stop along the way for burgers, don't you? Jeffrey's probably ready for some, and who knows when Sweetpea last ate? I know a drive-thru that is near a well-lighted picnic area. It'll give everyone a chance to stretch. I'm afraid, Lin, that you shouldn't have anything for now. You can have ice. Will that bother you?"

Lin shook her head. "I'm not in the mood for food, anyway." She had to admit to herself that he was the most considerate guy she'd met in a long while. Each time she found something positive about him, she reminded herself that he was just taking care of business, that the lieutenant was holding him responsible for her.

At the drive-thru, Craig ordered six burgers. "Leave the lettuce, tomatoes, and onions off four of them," he instructed, "and a cup with just ice, please." He turned to look at Jeffrey. "Nobody wants to see Sweetpea hungry or with onion breath," he teased. Turning back to Lin, he said, "Sorry to leave you out, but it isn't wise for you to eat anything until morning. Should you fall into a coma and vomit again, you could strangle yourself. When I get you settled at home, I will pick up some dry food for Sweetpea before I leave."

Lin nodded sleepily. "I've lost my appetite, anyway." She smiled, imagining how it would look as the four of them drove up with a motorcycle behind them, especially when Sweetpea leaped from the car. She figured Craig's good looks and considerate manner wouldn't be lost on Mom. He seemed so Southern for a Connecticut Yankee.

As she suspected, the Hills rushed out to greet her with expressions of bewilderment mixed with relief. Craig briefly explained to them the chain of events. "She needs to be awakened every few hours, Mrs. Hill, to be sure she hasn't slipped into a coma. If you don't feel you can do that, I will stay and see to her." He looked back to help Lin from the car.

Mrs. Hill looked past him at Lin. She made a silly expression and rolled her eyes. Her lips formed the word, "Whew."

Lin was not about to have herself thrown at Craig by her former in-law. "I can set my alarm," she offered, forming a silent "no way" toward Mrs. Hill.

Shrugging surrender, Mrs. Hill said, "No problem, doctor. I'll take good care of her for you."

Craig's eyes danced with mischief. Obviously, the little side-view mirror had shown him some of the gestures between Lin and Mrs. Hill. He leaned toward Lin and whispered so close to her ear that she shivered under his warm breath: "You're right; they're pretty cool." Loud enough for everyone to hear and in his strictly professional voice, he said, "I will call in the morning to check on you, but you should check in with your regular doctor tomorrow." He grinned. "Did I remember to say take two aspirin and call me in the morning?"

He asked directions to the nearest grocery or pet store and soon returned with a huge bag of dry dog food and a bowl the circumference of a basketball and four inches deep. It was definitely Sweetpea-sized. By that time, Mrs. Hill had tucked Lin into bed. He handed Mrs. Hill a business card. "Call me—anytime," he said.

Mrs. Hill smiled mischievously. "I'll put this here on Lin's bedside table—just in case."

While Craig was saying good-bye to Jeffrey and Sweetpea, Lin said, "Mom, I am so embarrassed. How could you throw me at him like that?"

The roar of the motorcycle faded into the distance. Mrs. Hill tucked the cover up to Lin's chin. "Somebody's got to do it! He's a keeper, Lin."

"He's a medical examiner, a coroner," Lin said, "just doing his job."

"He's gorgeous," Mrs. Hill said.

"He's STILL a coroner, whatever title they call him." Lin grinned. "Did you get a glimpse of those beautiful eyes?"

Mrs. Hill patted the pillow slightly. "Umm, and the

only thing they were looking at was you, dear."

Lin yawned. "He's just concerned about my injury. And he may be a licensed physician, but he is still just trying to help solve a murder, so forget it."

"I'll wake you in two hours," Mrs. Hill said. "But if you need anything meanwhile, I'm on the sofa. Just yell."

Tears trickled down Lin's face. "I just keep seeing Delia. It was horrible, Mom." She whimpered slightly. "They even took my fingerprints. It was as if they had already tried and convicted me."

"Now, Lin, you've seen enough shows and even edited enough mysteries to know they take everyone's fingerprints, just to be able to narrow it down to the real suspects. It's going to be all right. Especially with Craig at your side."

"Stop saying that, Mom! He's not at my side." Lin felt her eyelids growing heavy.

"We'll see, Lin. We'll see. Besides, you said you stopped outside the sliding glass door. Your prints won't even be inside at the murder scene. Now get some rest. As for me, it's time to introduce that oversized Sweetpea to Rouster, so ignore any sounds of mayhem in there. I am sure that both Sweetpea and Rouster can hold their own in a fight for top of the pecking order. The handsome doctor said the investigators probably will come tomorrow with more questions. You want to be fresh for them." She laughed. "And for Doctor Craig."

Lin pulled the cover up over her head. "I don't want to think about it. Or him! As a medical examiner or coroner, he's under the employ of their law enforcement. I think what you—we—mistook for . . ." Lin paused. ". . . for something else, is their version of good cop/bad cop. You've seen it on TV, Mom. One makes the suspect angry, and the other pretends to be a friend."

It didn't matter that Lin wanted sleep. She was stuck with the image of Delia lying in a pool of blood, staring. Everytime she shut her eyes, the image flashed back as fresh as when Lin first saw her.

As for suspects, anyone in Delia's life, past and present, might have done it. The subjects of her exposés were ruined; they probably hated her. They no doubt would be pleased to see her dead. What about the newest subject? That's probably the answer. But who had Delia selected for exposure this time?

So Delia's manuscript was a little late, Lin thought. *I shouldn't take my job so seriously. I should not have gone there. Then it would have been someone else discovering the body. The paper boy perhaps. Or a deliveryman. Or that mousy little secretary, Dottie.*

Lin sat up suddenly, jarring her head with a sharp pain. Where was Dottie? She'd know who the subject of the book was. She must remember to tell Lieutenant Trey about Dottie tomorrow. At least that should get him off *her* back.

A nasty thought hit Lin. What if that gung-ho officer waited and came to the office to interview her? What if he led her away in handcuffs? Lin moaned. With all these visions dancing in her brain, she needn't worry about being awakened every few hours. There would be no sleep.

Lin figured she had a leg up on the investigation that Trey didn't. She knew that she didn't do it. Probably the only way to convince him of that was to find out who did.

"Why can't I just edit my books in my cozy little office and keep my nose out of my authors' businesses?" Before Lin could answer that question, she had fallen asleep.

CHAPTER 4

As long as Lin lay with her head flat on the pillow and didn't move, she didn't hurt. But when can anyone not move? Especially with those horrible images in her mind. Poor Delia. Who could have killed her so brutally? From the quick glance Lin got of the crime scene, it must've been a terrible struggle.

Mrs. Hill brought in the Sunday newspaper with some cranberry juice and coffee. "Toast and an egg over easy coming right up. Nothing in the papers about Ms. Dorrs. The lieutenant is probably keeping it quiet until they locate next of kin or something." She scooted Rouster aside and helped Lin to sit up in the bed.

"Or until they arrest me," Lin said grimly. "I don't think Delia had any kin, at least none she ever admitted to." For a woman who exposed everyone else's underside, Delia kept her own life covered quite well.

Jeffrey bounced cheerily into the room and leaped

onto the bed. It was all Lin could do to keep from screaming. It felt as if each bounce was a hit to her head. "Jeffrey, please. Mom has a terrible headache. Don't bounce, sweetheart."

Lin held her head as a rush of fawn brown galloped into the room and leaped onto the bed with all fours. The silly face of the Great Dane grinned at Lin. Rouster, who had resettled himself on the bed, growled, assumed a defensive position, and spat a mighty *Pfttttttt!*

"Oh, mercy. I forgot about you for a few glorious moments." Lin felt as if her head might explode then and there.

Sweetpea ignored Rouster as if he didn't exist and planted a wet slurping tongue across Lin's cheek. She laughed despite herself.

"I dressed myself," Jeffrey said proudly. He was wearing a plaid shirt and striped pants that looked as if they were in a battle for dominance.

Lin smiled and tousled his hair. "I can see that. You sure you didn't get fashion tips from Sweetpea?"

"Grandpa will take care of Jeffrey today, and I'll stay with you," Mrs. Hill said. "I don't think you should be alone." She grinned mischievously. "The good doctor has already called this morning to see how you're doing. I told him your regular physician was not available, and that I was concerned about you. I think he's coming to check on you."

"Mom, you didn't!" Lin eased back on the pillow. "It's only been two years since the divorce. What are you doing to me?"

Mrs. Hill shrugged. "Two years too long. Gerald is in California with his teenage bride, and you and my grandson are here and alone. You were meant for a complete and loving family. I want to see you happy, Lin."

Lin patted her hand. "Gerald's wife Kiki is nearly twenty-three, and I *am* happy, Mom. I couldn't ask for better support than you and Dad." Sometimes she almost convinced herself of that.

Mrs. Hill laughed. "I don't know about that! Craig looked as if he was supporting you pretty well yesterday. He seemed to be enjoying it too."

Lin felt her face grow warm. This was ridiculous. She was 32 years old, a career woman with a responsible job at Indeco Publishing. She was no schoolgirl to be blushing over a little attention from a dreamy-looking guy.

"Jeffrey, why don't you and Sweetpea find Grandpa? I think he wants to take you two to the park for a run," Mrs. Hill said. When he had left, she said, "That lieutenant also called. He wants to talk to you, he said, while details are still fresh in your mind. I told him not until your physician said it was all right."

Lin placed her fingers on her forehead and temples and massaged gently. "I guess I should get it all over with as quickly as possible. The sooner I do, the sooner I can try to wipe it from my mind. I mean, this woman was not some stranger on the ten o'clock news. I *knew* her."

Mrs. Hill patted Lin's shoulder. "Craig will be here in a little while. Rest until I bring in your breakfast."

When Mrs. Hill had left, Lin retrieved Craig's business card from her bedside table. It had voice, fax, and pager numbers. Her eyes still didn't focus completely on the type, but he had more letters after his name than the alphabet: M.D., Ph.D., D.D.S. Beneath that, it said, Associate Medical Examiner: Forensic Pathology, Anthropology, and Odontology. Talk about an over-achiever and overqualified.

Lin closed her eyes. She fought the tingly excitement she felt, anticipating Craig's arrival. She liked looking at him. He was attentive, gentle, concerned. He was the medical examiner—a nice name for a coroner—and employee of the state, she reminded herself. He may be trying to build her trust in hopes of getting information—or a confession. Why should she trust him? She'd trusted once; she would not be so gullible again. Her eyes fluttered, and her breathing became even. She slipped into a meadow of Texas bluebonnets, nodding in a warm summer breeze.

"Lin?"

She blinked, trying to make herself leave her sweet dream. There were those beautiful blue eyes gazing steadily at her. Was that why she thought of bluebonnets? "Hi," she said.

"Hi, yourself," he said, grinning at her. He pulled a small penlight from his pocket and held one of her eyelids open, then the other. "Reflexes have improved," he said. "Follow the light with your eyes only. Don't move your head." He moved the light left and right, then up and down. "Not bad," he said. "Not bad at all."

"Then I can go to work tomorrow?" Lin asked.

"I didn't say that!" Craig said. "Look, I don't think I can hold Trey off the questioning, considering how fast you are recuperating. As much as I would like to give you some time to think this through—"

"There's nothing to think through!" Lin protested. "I just found her, that's all."

Craig placed his hand over hers, gently shushing her. "Calm down; you don't want to upset yourself. I should have said 'remember all the details.'"

Logic was telling her to jerk her own hand away, but

she ignored logic in favor of the warm, tingly feeling.

"Trey takes his job a little too seriously sometimes, but he doesn't railroad anyone just for an arrest." He grinned. "Besides, he's got to get through me on this one. You're my patient until you declare otherwise."

Lin smiled at him and placed her other hand on top of his. "Thanks." Those eyes! As blue as any lake, and they looked directly into hers. She felt as if she could fall into them and drown. Drown? Drown, autopsy, *coroner*. Lin shuddered.

"Are you all right?" Craig asked.

She nodded. "Just an involuntary shudder. Papa used to tease us, saying, 'Fox ran over your grave.'"

Craig fished in his black bag and pulled out his blood-pressure kit. "Tell me about yourself, Lin. It's really impressive since Spanish is your first language that you became such an expert in English that you are an editor. English is a difficult language to master. *Wood* and *would*, *read*, *read*, and *red*, *through* and *though*."

Lin bristled. She knew, after her speech classes at UT, that she had no trace of a *tejano* accent. "Why do you assume that Spanish is my first language? Because I'm Latino?"

"No, because you were muttering in Spanish while you were unconscious. You said, 'Lots of blood! Call the doctor! I'm scared. Let's go.'"

Lin stared at him. "If I was speaking Spanish, how do you know what I was saying?"

"You said, '¡*Mucha sangre! ¡Llame al doctor! Tengo miedo. ¡Vámonos!*' That's right, isn't it?"

"You speak Spanish? I'm impressed!" Lin said. And, she might have added, a little surprised and delighted. She shouldn't have been surprised, considering his degrees.

"*Sí, un poco*, a little," he said. "I took two years in high school, and remember, we doctors use a lot of Latin to dazzle our patients. It's not a very big gap between the two languages."

He touched his fingers to her pulse and kept his eyes on his watch as he spoke. "And I admit, I was trying to impress you. If my Spanish doesn't work, I can strum a mean flamenco and a little country and western on that old guitar I saw in the living room. Or if that doesn't awe you, I'm prepared to do 50 push-ups without falling on my face. But we're off the subject. I asked about you." He released her wrist. "A perfect 70."

Lin was a little surprised it hadn't shot up at that moment. She was more than impressed. She was intrigued. "Bet you say that to all your patients."

Craig laughed. "No, only very old ladies and pretty young women who throw up on my shoes at murder scenes."

The ease with which he spoke delighted her. She had practiced long and hard to appear at ease with people, even when she wasn't; it took a bit of pretending. "There isn't much to tell. My parents were born in Mexico. I was born in Texas but heard little English spoken until I attended school when I could. We went from farm to farm, picking whatever was in season. If not for my parents, I suppose I'd be there yet. They made sure we studied, even when we were moving about. I took a GED test, got an academic scholarship, and worked my way through college. Then I came to New York and, as they say, the rest is history."

Craig placed the stethoscope over her heart. "How did you meet your husband?"

Lin shifted uncomfortably. "Ex-husband," she reminded him. "He worked in the building next to mine. A mutual friend introduced us. We married too quickly. Except for our love for Jeffrey, we have nothing in common, and it ended." That was all she intended to say. Gerald's roving eye and Kiki were nobody else's business. It took her two years to admit it was over, and another two years to recognize that it was not her fault. She wasn't sure yet that she trusted her own judgment in people.

"The Hills seem like really great people," Craig said. "Strong heartbeat," he added, removing the stethoscope.

Lin laughed. "Yeah, I got custody of them in the divorce. What about you? You said you live alone. Ever been married? Kids?"

Craig shook his head. "Neither yet. There were four years in college for a bachelor's degree, which I cut to three; four years in med school; another five in anatomic and clinical pathology; and a year of residency. It hasn't left much time for relationships." He added, "Guess I've been waiting for the right one to come along."

She raised an eyebrow. "I saw all those degrees on your card. You've packed a lot of studies into so few years. You're what—32, 33? You know the statistics on our chances for finding the right one, as you put it? And how will you recognize her when she comes?"

"I'm 34 and an optimist, and I'll recognize her. She's intelligent, stable, has a sense of who she is, is not afraid of a lifetime commitment, and likes kids. I want what we all want, I guess: someone to love and who'll love me." He grinned. "I'd make the perfect husband; I would never bring my work home," he teased.

"Ooh," Lin said. "That's bad." She laughed despite herself.

Lieutenant Trey's big body filled the doorway, and he was staring at them without expression.

Behind him, Mrs. Hill shrugged. "Sorry," she said.

Craig stood up to greet him. "I don't recommend that you talk to her just yet. There is still some irregularity in the dilation of her pupils indicating—"

Trey stepped into the room. "She seems chatty enough, though. Rumors are already flying about Miss Dorrs's demise; our little community is up in arms, scared that there's a murderer among them. They need reassurance that it is isolated and personal."

"It's all right, doctor," Lin said. She was careful not to call him Craig in front of the lieutenant. "The sooner I talk to him, the sooner I can get my life back to normal." She paused. "What makes you believe that it is an isolated and personal murder, and not some burglar or—" She stopped. It might boomerang right back to her.

Trey cleared his throat. "I am not at liberty to discuss an ongoing investigation with—with you."

Lin narrowed her eyes at him, studying his placid face. She knew what he had started to say: *with a suspect.*

Craig scowled at Trey from beneath his thick brows. "I'm staying then," he said, looking at Lin, "to assure that my patient isn't overtaxed or upset. She is still quite exhausted and needs her rest."

Trey pulled the vanity chair up near the bed. "Stay then. But stay out of it."

Lin fluffed her pillows a bit, partly for comfort, but mostly to stall, to get her emotions under control. "Have you spoken with Dottie Dinwiddie?" she asked.

"Dottie Dinwiddie?" Trey asked. "Who is she? Does she live on the premises?"

"She is—was—Delia's secretary; I'm pretty sure she doesn't live on the premises. But she has an office there—that little summerhouse out near the pool. What if she has been kidnapped or murdered too?"

Trey frowned. "She worked weekends too?"

Lin shrugged. "I suppose not." However, it was odd,

considering the deadline for her manuscript, that Dottie wasn't working as many hours as it took.

"Are you saying you think Dottie could have murdered Delia?" Lieutenant Trey asked.

Lin shook her head. "No! I didn't say that at all! Dottie is fortyish, quiet, small, and in obvious awe of Delia. No, I don't think she could have murdered Delia; however, she might have a good idea who did, since she would know the subject of the next book."

"Fill me in," Trey said.

"Delia wrote unauthorized biographies of public figures," Lin explained. "She was a no-holds-barred biographer. No secret was too buried or too dark for her. It can't be comfortable knowing that your worst secrets will be public knowledge. Dottie could be in danger too, if she isn't dead already."

"You're the editor," Trey said. "And you don't know who the subject is?"

Lin shook her head. "I haven't received the manuscript yet. To avoid leaks, I get the entire manuscript on disk and send it directly to the printer. The titles are always teasing but never revealing. However, the subject is bound to know that he's the target by that time. Everyone in his or her past and present has been interviewed in depth. I imagine that someone would tell the subject that the book was about him."

Craig took a deep breath and let it out slowly. "A living autopsy."

Lin cringed at those two words, *living autopsy*; they cut to the heart of Delia's books. "I guess. But it's always verified truth, and it's always people who have benefitted personally and done harm to the public." She knew she was rationalizing; the truth was, it made money for the company and kept her in a top editing job at Indeco. She gazed at Craig. At least his autopsies were on the dead who couldn't be hurt anymore.

"Can you think of anyone else?" Trey asked.

"No, not really; that is, I guess not. Delia was not an easy person to get along with. Her ego trampled everyone—the paperboy who didn't come on time, the florist who sent the wrong color roses—everything made her angry."

"When did you start working with Ms. Dorrs?" Trey asked.

Lin stared at her hands. She needed a manicure. "I took over her books while her editor, Brad, was—was, er, in detox. Brad Benton, that is; he'd had some problems, but he's all right now."

"Then why are you still editing Miss Dorrs's books?" Trey asked.

"She liked the way I edited. And maybe she liked that I refused to take her verbal abuse the way Brad did; she liked the challenge. After Brad returned to work, Delia refused to work with him. Indeco agreed to her terms."

Lin grimaced. In one breath, she had given a co-worker a motive for murder. She and Brad weren't the best of chums. He knew about Gerald and Kiki before she did, and he had delighted in telling it to everyone else first.

Lin quickly added, "But it was all right with Brad; Delia was very difficult."

Lin let out her breath in a disgusted sigh. Now she had admitted that she didn't always get along with Delia. She had volunteered herself to the list of those with a motive for murder.

CHAPTER
5

Lin closed her eyes. "I'm really very tired. I can't think clearly," she told Trey. She feared the more she said, the more trouble she was putting herself in. And what was the alternative? Making the lieutenant suspect Brad just because he'd lost Delia as an author? She wanted to prove her innocence without pointing the finger at innocent bystanders.

Craig said, "Trey, I insist that this interview must stop right now. Maybe you should start a search for Dottie Dinwiddie instead of interrogating Lin, er, Ms. Hill."

As Trey spoke, there was ice in his tone. Lin opened her eyes to study him. "Don't tell me how to investigate, Gleason, and I won't tell you how to autopsy. What have you found so far?"

Craig glanced at Lin, then nodded toward the door. He stepped outside the bedroom and spoke in low tones. Lin strained to hear what he said.

"*Algor mortis*, cooling of the body, was 2 degrees Fahrenheit, indicating that she was killed within an hour of the boy's call to us. Death was due to two consecutive blows to the head with an irregular-shaped instrument of undetermined origin," Craig said.

"I am sure that I will be able to provide the match for that when the time comes," Trey said.

"The first blow to the temple was enough to cause unconsciousness. The second blow was at the base of the cerebellum." He pointed to the nape of his own neck.

"Another thing," Craig said. "Her wrists and ankles show signs of bruising, maybe a day old. And there were small traces of rope fiber embedded in her skin. She was apparently tied up for some time. However, stomach contents showed that she had eaten within two hours of her death. Lettuce and carrot portions as well as green pepper and celery were present and not yet digested."

"She was fed and murdered while bound?" Trey asked.

"I don't think so. It appears that she was tied for a while, perhaps bargained her way out of the bounds, then was killed in a struggle. Also, defense bruises. There were slight traces of skin under her nails. There may be enough for DNA testing. But that will take weeks to do."

Trey said. "I don't need weeks to arrest the killer."

Craig's voice raised slightly. "Trey, don't rush to judgment. I'll stake my reputation on this one. Maybe this Dottie Dinwiddie figured she was next. She may have gone into hiding. Find her, and she can provide you with some critical evidence and some genuine suspects."

Lin felt her skin crawl up her arms and spine. She was right. Trey did suspect her. If it weren't for Craig, she could be in a cell right now.

Trey's voice was even, calculating. "Staking your reputation may be exactly what you're doing, Craig."

Craig's voice softened. "Trey, let me take Ms. Hill to the crime scene as soon as she is able to get out of bed. Maybe she'll remember something that she's burying right now. She's not used to seeing things like that, the way we are. I'm responsible for the integrity of the crime scene."

"You can bet on that, Gleason. Totally responsible!" Trey stuck his head back into the bedroom. "I will want a complete list of all Ms. Dorrs's subjects for biographies, past and present, by the end of the day." He stalked out, and the front door slammed.

Craig wrapped his fingers around Lin's wrist. "Your pulse is too rapid. Lie back and rest. We'll talk when you're calmed."

Lin snapped, "How can I be calm? He's practically accusing me of murder!"

"He's frustrated," Craig said, gently brushing dark strands of Lin's hair from her face. "A murder, especially one where the murderer doesn't instantly confess, ruins his day. When he calms down, he'll come around." He tucked the blanket up under her chin. "When you can walk without feeling as if your head is going to fall off, I'll take you back to the estate. Maybe it will jog your memory."

Lin shivered at the thought of seeing Delia's place again. Even with Craig at her side, it was too awful to think about. "You're leaving now?" She had hoped he'd linger awhile. She enjoyed his company.

Craig grinned. "I think I'll go looking for a little boy with a dog as big as a pony. His grandpa might be needing a relief by now."

Lin smiled and closed her eyes. She had to admit, coroner or no coroner, he was a pretty neat guy. Not many bachelors would get along so well with a little boy. She had seen grown men flee in terror at the mere mention of her child. *Get hold of yourself, Lin. Remember? Good cop/bad cop? It could be a routine. Now where are those bluebonnets?* She desperately wanted to return to that peaceful vision of a Texas prairie with flowers covering the ground like a snug blanket.

When Lin awakened later, Mrs. Hill was standing at her bed with a tray for lunch. Chicken broth, a salad, and freshly baked rolls. Craig's conversation with Trey flashed into her mind. She'd never view salad in the same way again. The bud vase with the single red rose made her smile.

"Craig's idea," Mrs. Hill said, beaming. "It's from the bush in the front yard."

"Forget it, Mom," Lin said. "I can't get past the fact that he looks inside dead people's bodies and heads." She shivered involuntarily.

Mrs. Hill laughed. "If I were twenty years younger— all right, make that thirty—his occupation would be the farthest thing from my mind. He reminds me of that actor—what's his name?"

Lin shook her head. "I have no idea who you're talking about. And you were married thirty years ago with a child," she reminded her.

"So make me admit my age," Mrs. Hill teased. "But I still say he's a keeper."

The front door slammed and Lin braced herself for the onslaught of boy and dog. But the two walked into the room calmly. Sweetpea sat at the foot of the bed and rested his chin on the edge, looking wistfully at Lin. Jeffrey tiptoed in and whispered. "How are you feeling, Mom?"

Lin raised an eyebrow in question.

Craig winked. "The three of us had a little talk about how to take care of you."

"Sweetpea too?" Lin asked incredulously.

"He just needed to understand."

Lin laughed. "Next you'll agree that he is a vital witness to the crime."

Mrs. Hill said, "We'll leave Lin to feed herself. Come on into the dinette, Craig, Jeffrey. We'll have our lunch in there. You too, Sweetpea," she said. "I'm sure there's plenty of food for you too."

Sweetpea trotted off with Jeffrey.

Craig lingered. "Eat it all, especially the broth. You need your strength."

"Yes, doctor. Now go!" she said, waving him toward the door.

As she ate, she thought back over Delia's biographies she had personally edited. A washed-up movie star who had just started a comeback when Delia did an exposé of her questionable past. No, she had since died of a drug overdose. Then there was one on a broker who thought he could get away with insider trading until Delia dug up the goods on him. He was in prison. There was an architect who had been getting paid by the mob for years to let them bury a few enemies in the concrete foundations of his buildings. He was still serving time in prison. If the mob didn't go after her, who would?

Lin was sure it wasn't a random intruder looking for jewels and money, although Delia had flashed enough jewelry and wealth in television interviews. Her home was even featured on that show about rich and famous people. Lin felt that the murder had to do with the new subject for her manuscript. Dottie should know—if she wasn't dead too.

As Lin recalled from a visit there several years ago, Delia had a computer—two of them, in fact. One in the main house and one in the summerhouse, which Dottie used. Delia didn't type, however. She hand wrote her notes on legal pads. And she couldn't spell worth a darn. It was Brad who had insisted that she get a secretary. He had even found Dottie for her.

Poor Dottie; she could be lying dead out there in all that wooded area, or perhaps she was hiding, too frightened to show her face. Of course, Delia's death was known only by word of mouth this weekend, since the media hadn't gotten wind of it yet. If Dottie hadn't heard, she'd show up for work Monday morning none the wiser. It could be a terrible shock to her. Reading of Delia's death in the paper would be no easier for Dottie. The lieutenant wouldn't be able to keep it from the press much longer.

Lin set the tray aside. She snatched a pair of fresh jeans and a T-shirt that draped over the chair. She managed to dress herself without passing out. Encouraged, she put on socks and tennis shoes. When Craig returned to the room, she was sitting on the side of the bed, fully dressed. "I want to go to Delia's," she said. "Let's get this over with." She wavered slightly as she tried to stand.

Craig said, "You should wait at least another day."

"Tomorrow is Monday," Lin said, "and I intend to go to work. Today I need to do this. What if the trail grows cold?"

Craig grabbed her shoulders as she wobbled slightly. "You're in no shape to go to work. As for cold trails, you watch too many detective shows," he said. "Now lie down for your own good, please."

"No!" Lin said. "I want—need your help. But it has to be now, Craig." If she didn't go back now, she might not have the nerve later, she figured.

"You are one independent woman! Mrs. Hill!" Craig called. "Can you talk some sense into her?"

Mrs. Hill came to the bedroom door and shrugged. "Sorry, Craig. I think her mind is made up. Maybe going back will help the case. Maybe it will at least help her to start to put this into perspective." She smiled at the both of them. "I know you won't let any harm come to her."

Lin shot her a wicked glance.

"Okay," Craig agreed, shrugging. "I'll leave my motor here, and we'll take your car. I'll drive."

"You get no argument from me," Lin said.

"Oh, right," Craig said. "As long as I agree with you."

Lin grinned. "Now you're catching on."

With his arm wrapped around her, steadying her, she slowly descended the steps, being careful not to jar her head more than necessary. He helped her into the passenger side. She waved at Jeffrey as they pulled away.

"Lean back and rest," Craig told her, "and leave the driving to me."

"Yes, sir," she said. "Anything you say, sir."

He grinned. "Yeah, right! We'll see about that."

Lin dozed off, and she didn't awaken until the car wheels kicked up gravel. She found herself facing the tall iron gates with the brass D's on them. The drive was blocked with the yellow glow tape: CRIME SCENE DO NOT CROSS POLICE LINE. She felt a chill creep up her spine. *You can do this, Lin. You can do this.*

A state police car was parked just inside the gate. Craig got out, spoke with the officer, and signed a paper saying they had been at the scene. The officer opened the gate, and Craig drove the car up to the house where Delia's red convertible sat gathering a layer of dust. The house looked cold and uninviting.

Craig opened her door and said, "You'll have to wear protective coverings—cap, mask, cloth shoe covers, jumpsuit. I'll get them; wait here."

"I thought everyone had already gone over everything," Lin said when he returned.

"Yes, but we may return and try a few more times, just to be sure," Craig said. "Every criminal leaves something behind and takes something with him from a crime scene. Shed skin cells, a hair, maybe a rug fiber from his home or car, that sort of thing," he explained. "Criminals have been convicted on just such evidence."

He handed her latex gloves. "Here, these too. We wouldn't want you leaving any prints inside, would we? After all, you're on file now," he reminded her. He waited. "Ready?"

She nodded. "As ready as I'll ever be."

Craig removed the crime-tape seal and slid the patio door open. A myriad of odors drifted through the opening—blood, forensic chemicals, death. Lin tried to avert her eyes from the floor, but the large dark stain and the chalk outline of a crumpled body were like a magnet. A low moan grew into a loud wail. Her breath came in short gulping gasps, and she felt dizzy.

Craig's strong arms wrapped around her. "You're hyperventilating, Lin. Breathe deeply through your nose—hold it, now let it out slowly through your mouth. Again. Take it easy."

Without thinking, Lin hugged herself to Craig, weeping uncontrollably into his chest.

CHAPTER
6

Craig's arms wrapped around Lin like a protective blanket, holding her so close that she could hear the beating of his heart. He rested his chin on her head and kept repeating, "Breathe slowly, Lin. Deeply through the nose—hold it—blow out slowly through the mouth. Slowly. There is nothing here that can hurt you."

She closed her eyes and breathed deeply as he instructed. She could smell his talcum powder and aftershave lotion. It reminded her of Papa on Sunday, smelling as sweet as a baby and so handsome with his dark skin against his embroidered white shirt. His wedding shirt, he called it. Lin's breath slowly returned to normal.

"Second cozy scene of the day," the familiar voice said. It was Lieutenant Trey, standing at the sliding glass door, his arms crossed in that same defiant, show-me angle Lin felt he reserved just for her. He wore all the protective clothing except the gloves and shoe covers.

Lin reluctantly pushed herself away from Craig. "Thanks. I—I'm okay now. I guess I just lost it when I saw that outline and stain on the carpet. It was as if I was seeing it all over again, with Delia lying there." She dabbed at her eyes with the sleeve of the jumpsuit. "Sorry."

Trey slipped on latex gloves and shoe covers before entering. "Are you sure you're all right now?"

Lin took a deep breath. "I—I think so."

"Then look around. Tell me if anything is missing," Trey said.

"I'll try, but I was here only once, and that was two years ago. I don't think I'm the right one to ask this," Lin said. "Have you found Dottie yet?"

"No," Trey said. "Her landlord says that she hasn't been there for several days."

"Then she may be dead out there somewhere," Lin said.

"Or a suspect," Craig added.

Trey scoffed. "Or none of the above. I asked around the village, and the grocer said she mentioned she had a week off and would probably go on a brief motor trip. We left messages at her apartment for her to call when she returns. Perhaps she can shed some light on the motive. As far as I'm concerned, Miss Dinwiddie is not a suspect. We have our murder weapon, I believe, and it definitely did not come from her."

Craig said, "You have the murder weapon? Then why wasn't it sent to my lab for comparison with the wounds?"

"I've sent it to the FBI lab for confirmation. I want this case airtight. When I'm ready to make an arrest, I will," Trey said.

Lin thought it was strange that Dottie would have time off unless the manuscript was completed. In that case, it should be in her office Monday. Lin walked slowly around the room, trying to remember what it had looked like. Above the mantle was a large painting of Delia in a lavender evening gown. It showed a slim, beautiful platinum blond with a Mona Lisa smile. There were no telltale age lines about the eyes or hardness about the mouth. The hands showed long and elegantly manicured nails. Yet Delia was notorious for chewing her nails nearly to the quick. Surrounding the portrait were framed covers of her books, some of them hanging crooked as evidence of the struggle. "You asked about the subjects of her previous books," Lin said. "There they are, your lineup of suspects."

"Not a complete lineup, Ms. Hill," Trey said.

Lin chose to ignore his obvious meaning—that she too was a suspect. "You're right. We still don't know the subject for the next book, do we?" She moved along the bookshelves that held bound copies of Delia's books. They were shelved, not with the spines showing as most people did. Her books were face out so that the covers showed. The shelf below held videocassettes, each carefully labeled with the interview show it covered and the date of her appearance. It appeared that she had tapes of every interview she'd done.

On the mantle were small plaques and insignificant trophies, nothing major like a Pulitzer or American Book Award. Delia's house was her trophy. The house that secrets built. Lin walked into the next room with the two men following her.

"The computer," she said. "It's gone!"

"Are you sure?" Trey asked.

"This is the desk where it was. Delia was no typist. She might do a hunt-and-peck note now and then, but her secretary did the real typing." Her book jacket showed a photo of Delia working away on her computer. Lin knew it was strictly a publicity photo, though. She did everything by hand with poor penmanship and spelling. "See? There is a barely visible outline of where it sat. And see here. The printer is still here. The wire connectors are just lying there."

"Good eye for detail," Craig said.

"I'm an editor," Lin said. "That's what makes me a good one."

"I don't see any fingerprint dust on the connectors," Craig said. "A thief would have to grasp the connectors in order to release the computer."

"Burglary as a motive?" Trey asked. "Is that what you'd like me to believe? Why didn't the burglar take the printer then? And look around here. There's a TV, stereo, VCR, and the place fairly drips with expensive stuff. That doesn't make sense. I think the killer took the computer just to make it look like burglary was the motive."

Lin persisted. "And I think it just goes to prove what I've been saying all along. I think it has to do with her next book subject. That's what it's all about, I'm sure of it."

"Nonsense," Trey said.

"Did you check the summerhouse?" Lin asked. "Was there a computer there?"

Trey looked down at his feet. "No."

"No, you didn't check? Or no, there was no computer?" Craig asked. His voice held an edge to it.

"No, there was no computer," Trey shot back. "There are no computers anywhere on the property, okay?" Trey handed a clipboard to Craig. "This is the inventory of what is here, and what we took to the station. As you can see, there are no computers listed."

"Then doesn't that prove that someone was after the

manuscript?" Lin asked. "The two computers were networked. What was on one could easily be transferred to the other. Isn't it possible that the killer didn't know how to destroy the copies or didn't have time before I showed up? What if the killer knew that taking the computers wasn't enough? Maybe Delia, in an effort to stall and save her life, told him that there was a copy hidden somewhere. A hard copy would be nearly a ream of paper and difficult to hide. But a disk, maybe? Maybe that's why Delia was tied up. The killer was trying to get her to tell the location of the disk."

Trey narrowed his eyes at Lin. "That's pretty far-fetched. Besides, how do you know that she was tied up, unless you did it? Or did Gleason tell you? Do I have to call in an outside party to handle this investigation? One with no emotional involvement?"

"You were just outside my bedroom when you were talking," Lin shouted. "You think I don't have ears to hear?" She glanced at Craig. His arms were at his sides, but his fists were clenched tightly so that the latex gloves were tight over his knuckles.

"It is not emotional involvement; I am doing my job," Craig said. "And I'd suggest you do yours." His words were clipped and dripped with anger.

"I'm holding you responsible," Trey said. "I have photos and this inventory of everything here. Nothing is to be carried off, understand?" He snatched the clipboard from Craig's hands and stormed from the house.

Lin stood rigidly, watching Trey's broad body vanish from view. When he was gone, she sighed and stole a glance at Craig. She felt a mix of personal feelings just then. She was angry at Trey for his dogged determination to charge her with murder. And she was disappointed at Craig. He told Trey there was no emotional involvement.

Had she been misreading his signals? There was a small part of her that really wanted him to care about her as a person, not just as a witness in the crime investigation.

"He's ticked off," Craig said. "But Trey will check every pawnshop within a hundred miles, looking for those computers. It's going to be all right. Don't worry."

Lin laughed. "I'll bet that's what the captain of the *Titanic* said to the passengers too." She was beginning to have her doubts that everything was going to be okay. What if the computers weren't found? What if there were no other copies of the manuscript? And what if Dottie, the only other person who might know the subject, was dead?

Lin bit her lip, thinking. "Delia said she kept taped interviews with everyone as insurance against libel suits. She was meticulous about things like that, because sometimes people see what they said in print and it scares them. They go into denial. We should look for her audiotapes. I recall they were on those real small cassettes—you know, like miniature recorders. Maybe she kept them in a safe here or in a safety deposit box at her bank."

Craig and Lin searched the house and the summerhouse. They found tapes from previously published books but none for the forthcoming book.

"There's something I'm not remembering. Maybe if we watch one of the taped interviews, something will jog my memory. Do you think that's allowed?" Lin asked.

"Are you feeling all right?" Craig asked. "We can watch them here in the office on this VCR. We can't take the tapes out without signing them out, and I don't want to give Trey one more thing to grumble about."

"I'm with you on that," Lin said. "And I'm not at all tired." Perhaps her adrenaline was kicking in. It wasn't a lie. She did feel a bit better.

Lin curled up on the office sofa while Craig inserted the first cassette and turned on the television set.

Lin sucked in her breath as Delia's image appeared as big as life on the huge screen.

Craig sat down next to her and rested one arm on the back of the sofa, lightly gripping her shoulder. "Your shoulder muscles are tense. Relax. It's all right, Lin. Tell me if this gets too difficult."

Lin clasped her hands tightly in her lap. "I'm okay."

Delia was at her best, manipulating the questions into the direction she wanted to go. She seemed more in control than the poor interviewer. "I travel constantly for book signings but mostly for my research. I keep taped interviews of all my subjects and tattlers. They are perfect defenses in lawsuits."

Delia said, "I take notes too, to jog my memory as to what is on the tape. One rarely sees me without a legal pad in my hand. I believe in going to the hometowns of my subjects. Many times, an old schoolteacher or scout leader can give me an insight into the subject's personality before they became famous. I find that the subject watches to see what I write down and forgets that everything is on the tape."

"Of course," Lin said, hitting the pause button on the remote and freezing the figures on the screen in mid-sentence. "The notepads! Maybe the killer didn't know that Delia kept notes!"

Craig said, "Blank notepads were on the inventory, Lin. There was no mention of any written notes remaining here or taken into evidence."

"That can't be," Lin said. She leaped from the couch and wavered momentarily. She made a mental note not to make sudden moves until she was well. She rummaged through the desk drawers. The drawers seemed oddly empty. There were legal pads. But they were devoid of Delia's scrawling handwriting. One pad appeared slightly thinner than the other. Lin ran her hand across the top of the pad. She could feel the ridges beneath the green binding as if some pages had been removed. "Delia always took notes. She must've told the killer. He took them."

Whatever Delia had written was gone. Or was it? There were also slight indentations on the page, as if the pressure of a pen or pencil had gone through from the previous page. Lin snatched a pencil from the cup on the desk and rubbed over the indentations. As she did, writing appeared. "Craig!" she called. "Come here, quick!"

Craig hurried to her side, and she shoved the notepad into his hands. "See this? "It says 'Gory Alleluia.' I am willing to bet that that's the title of her next book."

"Weird title," Craig said. "Any idea about the significance?"

"Gory—bullfighting? Boxing? Ice hockey? Cockfighting? Any kind of blood sport, I imagine." She stopped. *Or perhaps autopsies? Coroners?*

"But Alleluia?" Craig said. "Praise, singing, worship, religion, church? Something to do with Easter?'

She sighed. "I can't think."

"What's this down here, just beneath that?" Craig asked, pointing. "Rub a little more here."

Lin studied the letters, shaking her head: *ds hows.* She shrugged. "I have no idea."

"D.S. Hows?" Craig said. "Or is that an *e* instead of an *s*? *Howe*, perhaps? Could that be the subject of her book? Douglas, Donald, DeWitt, Dennis?"

"I doubt it," Lin said. "Delia dealt only with really well-known public figures. Do you know anyone by that name? I've certainly never heard of anyone by that name.

She was no grammarian, but surely she'd use capitals if they were initials and a last name. She did for the title."

"Perhaps it's all one word, an odd name, like Dshows," Craig suggested. "Maybe if we pronounce it slower, or faster?"

"Dshows. Deee Shooows. Deee sssssss," Lin said. "Nothing."

Craig said. "Silent *h* perhaps? Dows, as in chemicals? Or—"

"I've got it!" Lin said. "Hows—hooows or house—ds house. She has never gotten the apostrophe straight. I think that is meant to be *d's.*" She sighed. "But what do we have when we know that? Delia's house? It's been searched and researched."

"And Dottie's house," Craig reminded her.

"And what is in d's house? Evidence? The manuscript? I feel as if we're moving farther from the truth instead of closer," Lin said dejectedly. She shoved the notepad back into the desk drawer and closed it. "Please, take me home. This is more depressing than helpful."

Craig replaced the videotape, and the two of them stepped out the back sliding door and removed their jumpsuits, gloves, and shoe covers. Lin snatched off the wretched mask and cap and tossed her head lightly. Her dark hair settled around her shoulders. She was suddenly aware that Craig was watching her, smiling.

"Sometimes truth is slow in coming, Lin, but it will come. Believe me," he said. He resealed the tape across the door.

Lin wanted to believe him more than anything. But doubts circled her brain like storm clouds.

"Just throw your disposable gear in that covered waste barrel," he instructed. "The forensics team may get desperate enough to vacuum our crime-scene covers, just to be sure they have everything."

When Lin got into the car, he said, "Why don't we stop at Roadhouse Steaks before returning home? I'll treat you to the best baked potato anywhere in the U.S., served in the presence of a great jazz quartet. You like jazz?"

Her first instinct was to say no. She overcame it. "I'd like that."

Craig stopped the car at the gate and signed them out with the deputy. Turning onto the road, he said, "We are going to have to stop for gas too. I think the tank is running a little low unless your gas gauge is not accurate."

"Okay. There's a charge card in the glove box." She leaned back with her eyes shut. Suddenly she sat bolt upright and shrieked.

CHAPTER 7

Lin was glad she was belted in, as Craig hit the brakes so fast that she surely would have sailed through the windshield of the Beetle.

"What?" Craig shouted.

"How could I have been so stupid?" she said. "The concussion must be blocking my thinking."

Craig leaned back and momentarily closed his eyes until his facial muscles relaxed. "Lin, you scared me half to death! What are you talking about?"

"When you mentioned needing gasoline, and I told you about the credit card, I realized how dense I'd been. Credit card equals a paper trail," Lin said. "Delia traveled constantly, and she had to keep records of every expenditure for tax purposes and for reimbursements where possible."

Craig nodded and shifted the gear to let the car start forward once more. "A paper trail," he repeated. "You mean you think the killer stole the credit cards and would be using them; therefore he can be followed?"

"That's possible, of course, Craig. But I mean that is how we can find out who the subject of her next exposé was. I feel so sure that when we do, we will find the murderer."

"There is no *we* in this, Lin. Be a witness. But don't start investigating. Leave that to Trey and to me. There is a killer out there. Besides, there were no credit card receipts listed on the inventory," Craig said.

"But that's impossible!" Lin said.

"Improbable, maybe," Craig said, "but I saw the inventory list myself, and I should mention, I have a photographic memory." He paused. "Ah, here we are. Roadhouse Steaks." He turned the car to the right and into a parking lot facing a two-story building of white stucco with brown wood trim. Trees and brush grew almost up to the sides and back. "You're going to love this place."

Lin doubled her fists in frustration. "Craig, how can you change the subject so quickly? This is important!"

Unbuckling his seat belt, he grinned at her impishly. "Because I'm hungry, that's how. Come on, Lin. Relax and think of yourself a few minutes."

He got out, came around to the passenger side, and opened the door, reaching in a hand. "Steady now."

Did he think that she was still so helpless? Lin wondered although she was hardly going to complain. "I am thinking of myself," Lin said. "Even if I were thinking only about the missing manuscript—and believe me, it is important to my job—I would want this solved. But, Craig, I don't want Trey pinning the murder on me because he can't think of anyone else."

Craig opened the door to the restaurant and allowed Lin to enter. "Trey has an irritating manner about him. But solving a murder isn't like the game of pin the tail on the donkey. Trey's like the tortoise."

"And you're thinking that I'm like the hare," Lin said.

"Two," Craig told the hostess. "Near the back window."

They followed the hostess to the small table at the rear of the room, which was nearly solid glass. It gave Lin the feeling that she was eating outdoors. Votive candles flickered on each table and reflected in the glass like clusters of stars. The tablecloths and napkins were a sage green, making the tables seem almost a part of the greenery outdoors. She suddenly felt underdressed and overoptimistic.

"You're in for a real treat," Craig said as they were seated.

"I usually dine out on burgers in Formica booths with paper napkins and my eight-year-old gentleman friend," Lin said. "Almost anything short of a drive-thru would be a step up. But this is very nice. I'm glad you brought me here." She became aware of movement in the underbrush. Lin held her breath as a doe and two spotted fawns glided into the clearing to a trough filled with corn. "Oh, my! Look how close they are." She almost wished that Jeffrey was here to see it too. On second thought, being with an adult male, especially one so charming and handsome, was quite satisfying for a change. Although she hated to admit it even to herself, she enjoyed this particular male's company.

"I thought you'd like this. Before we leave there'll probably be a few raccoons, maybe even a stag, coming to feed. It's the best floor show in town—next to the quartet here, that is."

The musicians filed onto the raised platform—a drummer, pianist, saxophonist, and bassman. Lin recognized the first strains of "Take the A Train." She smiled at Craig and nodded her approval.

The music was good, soothing background. The view was wonderful. And she was sitting across from a great-looking guy, who seemed unaware that women's heads had turned his way, because he was looking only at her.

He raised an eyebrow. "Penny for your thoughts, or has inflation made that a dollar?"

Lin unfolded her napkin and placed it in her lap, smiling to herself. *Not on your life, Dr. Craig Gleason,* she thought. *These thoughts are private, priceless, and even a little dangerous for a single mother.* "The airline, car rental, hotel, food receipts. They have got to be somewhere—unless the killer took those in an effort to hide his identity."

Craig's face crinkled in an expression of what must surely be disappointment. "Maybe everything goes to an accountant. Lin, let it go, at least for the duration of the dinner. How about a petite filet and one of their famous baked potatoes?"

Lin laughed. "Oh, you mean, stroke on a plate with heart attack on the side?"

"It doesn't hurt once in a while. Don't you get tired of chicken and fish and raw veggies? The only real substance you've had today was that broth, remember?"

"Aw, you noticed! I do tend to cluck and seek water," Lin said, laughing. "Why not? I'll return to my health food soon enough. Or I'll prepare us a Tex-Mex meal, guaranteed to clean out your arteries and sinuses." She turned toward the window, hoping there was a night visitor to interrupt the conversation. Had she just talked about cooking a meal for him? Had she just used the word *us?* She mentally kicked herself for even thinking it.

Craig ordered for the both of them. He leaned across the table and took her hand in his. "Lin, I promise you this. I will keep on Trey's back to solve this thing. I will keep him *off* your back as much as possible. I will inquire about the credit receipts, although I have no idea how that will tell you who the biography was about. Surely

Dottie will have all that information when she returns from her motor trip."

Lin placed her other hand on his. They had slipped so easily from Dr. Gleason and Ms. Hill to Craig and Lin. She enjoyed being with him, even under these circumstances. "Now, who's talking about the case? I'd completely set it aside until you reminded me!"

"Yeah, right. I could see that written all over your face," Craig said.

The waiter returned with glasses of iced tea. Lin jerked her hands back as if she'd been caught on the front porch with a date. She felt her face grow warm and was glad the lights were low. She'd had enough real dates since her divorce to not feel this jittery or uncomfortable. Was it his job or just his overwhelming charisma? She hoped she wasn't that childish or that starved for attention. "Oh, look!" she said. "There are a couple of raccoons now." She was happy to change the subject.

The waiter brought their green salads with the house dressing, slightly tart and icy cold. The aroma of freshly baked bread was too tempting to resist. She flung back the napkin covering the straw basket and offered it to Craig first. Buttering a half slice for herself, she said, "Unless Delia's subject grew up in Washington, D.C., or one of the larger cities, I believe I can figure out who it was. She always visited their hometowns. She went to their old colleges and courthouses. Maybe she got a parking ticket outside a courthouse or had a receipt from a cab in a small town. Remember, it is always someone famous now. And little towns like to brag on their successes—until Delia gets a hold on them, that is."

"Lin, if you ever want a second career, you might consider law enforcement," Craig said, laughing. "Your mind works like a good detective's."

"Elementary, dear Dr. Watson," she said. "Elementary. What about you? Did you consider another career ever? I mean, with live people?" She shifted uncomfortably in her chair. "Do you enjoy your work?"

Craig shrugged. "Enjoy? It is not work to enjoy, Lin. It's work that satisfies. I am good at it, so I have satisfaction and a feeling of accomplishment. Have you ever been to the morgue in New York?" he asked.

"No!" Lin said. "I hope I never have to!"

"There's an inscription in the lobby of the building: *Taceant colloquis effugiant risus. Hic locus est ubi mors caudet succurene vitae.* This isn't the exact translation, but basically it means 'Let conversation stop and laughter cease. This is the place where death delights in helping the living.'"

"Death and delights," Lin said. "Odd paradox."

"The dead speak to us if only we will listen," Craig said. "My interest has always been in forensics—every phase of it. You think that *medical examiner* is just a less frightening word for *coroner,* but we are different. A medical examiner is a licensed physician with additional training in forensics specialties and appointed or hired for his credentials. Coroners are mostly elected and don't even have medical degrees, let alone a specialty in forensics."

Craig toyed with his water glass as he spoke. "Last year in Connecticut alone, homicides accounted for 168 of the deaths. But we processed nearly 14,000 death reports, with over 11,000 of them warranting further investigation. That included, of course, over 7,000 scheduled for cremation. By law, we have to examine those; it's the last chance to answer questions. This year looks to be no better. The massacre at the lottery office in Newington didn't give us much challenge. But we've had a half dozen bodies or skeletal remains turn up in the East Haddam dam or woods, at a roadside in Southington, Westbrook, East

Windsor, Canton—it's as if the earth opened up and the unidentified dead are everywhere. Who are they? Was it natural causes, murder, accident, or suicide? If one of them were a loved one, you'd want to know, wouldn't you?"

This was hardly the conversation Lin had expected at the dinner table, especially in this romantic setting with a guy she felt genuine physical attraction to. Yet she was drawn by his intensity and by her need to understand it—and especially him. "I—I guess, but it is so invasive, so disrespectful of the dead, isn't it?"

"You're probably thinking of the full autopsy—the infamous 'Y' cut plus the skull and brain dissection. That's not always necessary, Lin. Mostly they consist of tissue samples, cultures, drawing of fluids, etc. You said it was disrespectful. I think disrespect is never knowing the truth. Can you even imagine the number of murders that go undetected—especially those of infants and children— because some politically elected coroner doesn't know a thermometer from a tongue depressor?"

He paused for a sip of water. "Sometimes the dead tell us more than the living. They make better witnesses. At least they don't lie. I can help free the innocent or aid in convicting the guilty. Even the long-dead give up their secrets. With my forensic anthropology computer enhancement I can create a face from even a partial skull. I can add years or take them away."

Craig shrugged. "I like knowing that I've given a family peace of mind or that I've given an identity to a John or Jane Doe with no more to go on than a skull or a jawbone with teeth. But you probably don't want to hear all this, especially now."

"Come on, you started this!" Lin insisted. "How can you know what someone looked like? A skull is a skull is a skull, right?" She remembered the celebration of the Day of the Dead, *El Día de los Muertos*, in her youth. Grinning skulls, skeletons—it is supposed to be a day to think happy thoughts about the deceased and to honor them.

Craig moved to the chair nearest her. He wrapped his hands around hers and traced across her forehead to the temples. Then he traced his own. "Feel? The flesh depth here is thin; it's a given." He traced just below her cheekbones with one hand and simultaneously he drew the other across his own. "Beginning here, and back to here, it's thicker—much thicker right here in the cheek hollows and here. Yet you can see that my face is broader than yours. Forensic anthropologists have measured thousands of people, male and female, all ages. They've determined the characteristic depths of tissue at various points on our skulls. These are the standards by which we measure now."

He leaned in close and ran his forefinger down the length of her nose and below. "The nasal aperture will tell me the width of the nose, and the bony depression here at the top of the aperture and here at the bottom of it gives me the length."

His face was close and his eyes followed their fingers as he traced her features. As if hypnotized, Lin locked her own eyes on his. For the first time she noticed minuscule white flecks in his blue eyes, like snow against a clear blue sky. She sucked in her breath.

"The size of your orbits—that bony frame around your eye sockets—determines the placement of the eyes." He outlined her lower lip with his finger. "I can tell how thick the lips would be by the length of the teeth." His eyes locked on hers. "Your hands are trembling. Did I upset you?"

Lin startled, realizing that she was staring open-mouthed at him. She had an almost irresistible urge to kiss him then and there. She blinked slowly, willing herself to break eye contact. "Wow," she breathed. This guy has absolutely no clue as to the effect he had on her or half the women in the room right now.

He grinned at her. "I feed the measurements into the computer, and it generates an approximate look. It's like playing connect-the-dots. Before, we had to use pins, glass eyes, modeling clay, latex paint. It was time consuming. These computer programs save months of work."

He moved back to his chair. "Given certain traits of the skull I can tell you the ethnicity. With the mineral content I can sometimes discover where they lived." He grinned those perfect rows of teeth at her. "Or give me a photo of a child, and I can show you what it will look like at 20, 60, or 80 years old, especially if I know what the parents looked like. Come by the lab, and I'll show you the future."

"No thanks," Lin said. "I don't want to know!"

He waved off her doubts. "You have nothing to worry about, not with your bone structure. It would be a pleasure to grow old next to you."

Lin's breath caught in her throat. She clasped her iced tea glass to hide the trembling. She cleared her throat; what was that lump? Her heart? "I can certainly better appreciate the work you do now that I understand it more. If I lapse back into childish superstitions, please be patient with me."

Craig reached across the table and wrapped his hand around hers. "Patience is one of my best traits." He released her hand and leaned back in his chair. "What if this subject for Delia's book was so hush-hush that she did everything by cash?"

Lin was shaken by the sudden shift in subject. She reluctantly dismissed her fantasies. "No, she wouldn't do that, not when she needs proof for taxes."

"There were no credit cards listed in the inventory. You'll have to wait until statements come to the house. I don't think you have that kind of patience," Craig teased.

"I know, I'm the hare. What if I'm right, and Dottie's dead?"

"Unless her body turns up, you have no more than a theory, and I doubt if you can convince Trey to go to a judge for a court order based on a theory," Craig reminded her.

Lin picked up her fork and turned it over and over in her hand, biting her lip. "I won't need a court order."

Craig leaned forward. "Computer hacking?" he asked. "Are you thinking about hacking into the credit card system? That's illegal, Lin."

"I barely know how to retrieve my own documents and to write e-mail," Lin scoffed. "How would I suddenly turn skilled hacker?" Lin didn't know how to hack, but she knew someone who did. And he owed her, big-time.

Meanwhile, she was determined to enjoy herself. The quartet finished "Take the A Train" and played the first bars of "Duke's Place." Good music, a drop-dead gorgeous guy who is bright, and delicious food. Lin could almost make herself believe that this was a real date. It was perfect—if not for a concussion, a murder rap hanging over her head, and her job possibly in jeopardy.

Then there was Craig—about whom she felt drawn in so many directions. Who was he really? The easygoing, fun-to-be-with Craig? The one who could charm little boys and big dogs into behaving and make single mothers' hearts beat faster? Or was he the passionate medical examiner just doing his job? Trust him, he said. Gerald had taught her that was a dangerous thing to do.

CHAPTER 8

It was nearly 10 P.M. when Craig pulled Lin's Volkswagen Beetle to a stop in front of her duplex. Jeffrey was sitting on the stoop crying into Mrs. Hill's shoulder. Lin dashed up the sidewalk. "What is it?" she asked. "Is he hurt? Why is he still up?"

Jeffrey turned a teary-eyed face toward her. "Mom, Mom, Sweetpea is gone! He ran away from home." Jeffrey wrapped himself around Lin's legs and sobbed pitifully.

Lin rubbed his shoulders, comforting him. "Oh, honey. I'm so sorry. How did he get away?"

Mrs. Hill stood. "From the looks of your apartment, Rouster and Sweetpea had a free-for-all. And Sweetpea took it out on a few of your stuffed pillows, I'm afraid. I scolded him and put him out in the backyard to separate the two of them. I guess he jumped the fence. I'm sorry. I should've considered a dog that big wouldn't stop at a three-foot fence."

"Grandma hurt his feelings," Jeffrey wailed, "and he ran away from home."

Mrs. Hill was near tears. "Jeffrey, I'm sorry. Grandpa is out looking for him."

Mr. Hill walked up the walkway about then, alone. "I called and called, but I didn't find him. I'll look again in the morning."

Craig squatted so that he was face to face with Jeffrey. "When I was about your age and had a dog, our family moved to a new house. And you know what? Dino ran right back to the old house twenty miles away. I bet that is exactly what Sweetpea is doing."

Jeffrey sniffled and wiped his face on his sleeve. "Do you think so?" He turned toward Lin. "Mom, let's go get him. He'll be so scared all by himself."

Lin glanced at Craig and shrugged. "Is that what you think, really?" Papa had never let the children have a pet because they were always on the move. Until she got Rouster for Jeffrey, her experiences with animals were through reading mostly.

Craig stood up. "Absolutely. That was home to him for a long time. But I doubt Sweetpea will make it there this soon. Tell you what, Jeffrey, I'll keep an eye out all the way home, and if I spot Sweetpea, I'll bring him right back to you."

Jeffrey looked at Craig with an expression of doubt. "You're on a motorcycle. You can't bring him back."

"Bet I can! I think that Sweetpea would love to ride on a vintage Harley. Of course, I don't have a helmet for him."

Jeffrey laughed.

Lin patted Jeffrey's cheek. "Craig will watch for him, and tomorrow before I go to work, I will go to Sweetpea's old house and see if he's there. You know, it will probably take him all night to get there anyway. Right now, you need to go get ready for bed. You have school tomorrow."

"But, Mooooom!"

"By the time you get home from school, I think that Sweetpea will be here, waiting for you. Now scoot."

Jeffrey hugged his grandparents and Lin. He looked at Craig. "You really will watch for him?"

"I really will."

"Thanks," Jeffrey said, and wrapped his arms around Craig in a warm hug before skipping into the house.

Craig grinned at Lin. "I could get used to that."

He had to be made up, Lin thought. As Mom said, he was definitely a keeper for someone. She suddenly felt tongue-tied, as if on a first date. And of course, it was no date at all; it was business, and the dinner was no more important than a business luncheon.

What date starts with a crime scene and ends on the sidewalk with her ex-in-laws standing there, grinning at her? "Thanks for calming Jeffrey. I hope we do find Sweetpea. I'm already getting used to that stomach on four feet."

"I suspect that he'll head home as the crow flies, rather than follow the road. But I will keep my eye out for him. You aren't supposed to go to work tomorrow, remember? That includes motoring off in search of runaway canines. Doctor's orders. Besides, the blood in that lump on your head is going to give way to gravity, and you're going to have one heck of a shiner starting tomorrow."

"Oh, great," Lin moaned. "Just what I need."

"Oh," Mrs. Hill said, "I forgot! I have some leftover pot roast I could heat if you two are hungry."

"Thanks, Mom, but we've eaten," Lin replied too quickly.

"Oh?" Mrs. Hill said. She grabbed Mr. Hill's sleeve and

pulled him toward their apartment. "It's late. Let's go in." As she turned, she winked at Lin.

Lin rolled her eyes. She just wished Mom wouldn't be reading into the situation something that wasn't there. She turned toward Craig. "Thanks for a beautiful ending to a perfectly lousy day."

"I'll talk to you tomorrow," he said. "Lin, please forget whatever you were thinking of doing about the credit cards. And don't even think about going to work tomorrow. Be patient."

"I'll think about not thinking about it," she said. And she would, all the way to the telephone, as soon as Craig left.

"Oh, and if, despite doctor's orders, you do come out our way—"

She grinned at him impishly. "That I won't think about." She was beginning to feel as if she were on an emotional roller coaster.

Lin startled as Craig leaned over and lightly kissed her cheek. Her face felt suddenly warm. She touched her cheek where he'd planted the kiss and smiled. *I could get used to that*, she thought. Lin was grateful for the dim light or else he'd see that she was blushing. What a nasty habit, blushing. It gave too much of your thoughts away. "Good night," she said. "Be careful going home on that thing. You know what they call them—*donor mobiles!*"

"I know what they call them. I'm a medical examiner, remember?"

Yes, darn it, she remembered. Try as she would, she couldn't put that out of her mind. Nor could she put that kiss out of her mind.

"It is also called a *hawg*," he teased.

She watched him as he started the motor with a rumble. He slipped on his helmet and buckled it under his chin. "'Night," he said. The streetlight reflected off his perfect, white teeth as he smiled at her.

Lin watched as Craig turned the Harley toward home and roared off, disappearing from view.

Lin rubbed her cheek, smiling. She straightened up. *He's just doing his job. Get that through your silly head.* Yet another little voice was saying, *Then why did he kiss you?*

As she climbed the few steps to her door, the Hills' door flung open. "Well?" Mrs. Hill said. "What do you think? Keeper, right?" She was grinning from ear to ear.

"Go to bed, Mom," Lin said. "And don't even think it!"

Mrs. Hill pretended surprise. "Why, I haven't any idea what you're talking about. Call me if you need me, sweetheart." She laughed and closed her door.

Inside, Lin looked around. Tufts of cotton and goose-down feathers from the pillows still clung here and there to the wall, the sofa, and the chair. Rouster was huddled on the back on the sofa, looking out of sorts. As Lin reached to pick a piece of cotton off him, he swelled his body and spat a loud *Pffffft!*

"Don't give me any lip," Lin scolded. "It was probably as much your fault as Sweetpea's." She tucked Jeffrey in for the night, then glanced at the clock. It was a quarter till eleven, still early in California. She dialed.

Gerald answered, and after Lin had asked about the health of Kiki, she said, "I have an important favor to ask. A big one."

"I'm listening," Gerald said. He must be learning; he didn't commit his help before hearing the favor this time.

"I need about six months' worth of credit card statements."

"No problem."

"For one of my authors."

"Ask her."

"No, you don't understand. I can't ask her. She's—she's dead."

"You sure have rotten luck with authors, Lin. First that one was carried off in a straitjacket, and now a dead one?"

"Tell me about it! Soon I'll have authors begging for a new editor! But it's really important, Gerald."

"If she's dead, you can't get into her statements unless her estate attorney gives them to you," Gerald said. "That information is awfully personal, Lin. Why do you need it?"

Hastily, she explained to Gerald her theory about the receipts.

"Lin, if what you say is true, then this deputy can get a judge to subpoena her statements. He could even convince a judge to get *your* phone records. You're calling from home, I assume."

"Yes."

"They would have this phone number and it wouldn't take a genius to figure out who provided you with the information. I can't do it, Lin. The equipment used to trace hackers is getting very sophisticated. I know, because I designed some of it myself."

Lin sighed. "I understand." She fought to keep the tears from spilling onto her cheeks. "I guess that's all; thanks anyway."

She consoled herself with a steamy hot bubble bath, and while soaking she had an idea. She quickly dried off and dressed for bed. Lin dialed one of her own credit card companies. She pretended she didn't remember her account number and didn't have her card with her. She asked if they could send her a copy of a lost statement anyway.

"I must have your social security number and your

mother's maiden name as a security precaution," the assistant said.

Lin hung up. "Yes!" she shrieked. "I can do this!"

"Mom?" Jeffrey called. "Was that Sweetpea coming home?"

"No, dear. Go to sleep now," Lin called.

She must go to the office tomorrow, despite doctor's orders. She would have every bit of information she needed there.

Lin realized she was smiling despite herself. She rubbed her cheek where Craig had kissed her good night. He was awfully good at calming Jeffrey too. She was more than a little attracted to him. *Forget it, Lin!* she told herself. *You are vulnerable right now. You are in need of a sympathetic shoulder—any shoulder would do.*

No matter, she thought. Tomorrow when she got those statements, she'd be well on the way to solving Delia's murder. Craig was quite another matter. She just hoped he wouldn't tell Trey what she was up to. He had asked her to trust him. Could she?

CHAPTER 9

The next morning, Lin stood in front of her mirror studying her image. Craig was right about the shiner. It was going to be a beast with shades of indigo and mauve. How charming. Well, a little extra foundation and her best sunglasses would have to do. She was anxious to get to work and try out her theory on Delia's credit cards, but she had promised Jeffrey that she would return to the Dorrs estate to look for Sweetpea.

For now she wore dark-blue slacks and a matching sweatshirt in case she had to go crawling around dragging the overgrown beast into the car. Lin spotted Craig's business card on her bedside table; she placed it in her wallet.

She waited until Jeffrey was on the school bus before leaving. With any luck she could locate Sweetpea on the outside, trying to get in. She did not look forward to facing that place again, especially alone. *Don't be a baby,* she scolded herself. *You are not going to turn into one of those weepy sorts who need strong arms to protect her.*

73

Sure enough, she spotted Sweetpea outside the big double gate, and he was howling miserably. The young officer was nearly beside himself, trying to shush him.

"Don't you dare jump up on me, Sweetpea," Lin scolded. "I am very upset with you. Get in the car right now." By the time she pulled out of the driveway and back onto the road, the officer was having laughing fits.

Back at the duplex, Lin shoved him inside and warned him and Rouster to call a truce while there was no referee to see to them. She changed into a black sheath, tied a colorful scarf about her hips to detract from her face, and inspected herself in the mirror. Dog and cat hair clung to the dress already. It'd have to do. She grabbed her sunglasses and purse and scooted out to the little Beetle. This would be its first time into the city, but she didn't have time to fool with public transportation today.

Lin parked in a downtown garage and walked the distance to Indeco. She greeted Roland, the security guard, in the lobby near the elevators and rode up the five floors. Marilyn, the receptionist, was on the phone but buzzed her through before she could fish her security card from her purse.

Lin kept her eyes straight ahead and trotted through the maze of halls toward her small office near the back. She was in no mood to have anyone asking her about the sunglasses. Bess looked up from her paper, shook her head sadly, and raced off to the coffee machine. By the time she returned, Lin was settled at her desk.

"I was so sorry to hear about Ms. Dorrs," Bess said. "What a shock. Must have been to you too. You've been crying, huh?" She motioned toward the sunglasses.

Lin startled. "It was in the papers this morning?"

Bess shook her head. "Oh, no. Not a word. Isn't that odd? Brad told me."

Lin accepted the coffee Bess offered and thanked her. First, she took a sip to gather her thoughts. How did Brad find out if it wasn't in the papers? Had Dottie told him? She always stopped off at Brad's cubicle when she came to the building. They were probably good friends, especially since it was he who got her the job. But if she knew, then she was not on a motor trip. Why hadn't she come forward? Was she still too frightened to do so? And why had she informed Brad? Trey had successfully kept it quiet for two days, except for rumors, but word had leaked out.

"Anything in the mail or by courier?" Lin asked. She was secretly hoping that the disk with Delia's manuscript had made it to her desk by now, although she felt a bit guilty about that. She could rationalize that it would help solve the murder, but the truth was, she was starting to panic that the big dollar advance was for nothing.

"No," Bess said. "Nothing that can't wait." Bess frowned at the sunglasses. "I could bring back a cucumber from the company dining hall. They work wonders in soothing and shrinking puffiness."

Lin slowly slid the glasses off. "No, I—I had a minor accident. The bump on my head is draining into my eye."

Bess gasped. "Oh, dear! It looks really bad! Did you see a doctor?"

Lin's face spread into a grin at the thought of Craig. "Oh yeah, that I did. But never mind this. What else did Brad say?"

"Not much, just that she was apparently killed by an intruder. He was terribly shaken. I guess, despite the bad blood between them, he really cared."

Lin tapped the edge of her desk with her pencil. "Well, there are other books to be edited, Bess. I'd best get to work now. Oh, Bess, just don't mention my eye to anyone else, okay?"

She busied herself, rearranging paper on her desk, and

Bess turned to leave. "Oh!" Bess said, "I almost forgot your phone messages." She retrieved them from her own desk and brought them to Lin.

"Thanks, Bess. That's all for now," Lin said. She hastily thumbed through her messages. Someone in Wyoming called to invite her to speak at a conference in July. An author called to see why she hadn't gotten her page proofs yet. And Dr. Craig Gleason called. He left no message. Lin buzzed the intercom. "Bess, will you call the fellow in Wyoming and get some details about what he expects me to do and a specific date for the conference?"

Jeffrey would be with the Hills in California in July, visiting Gerald. She knew she'd be at loose ends without them, so the conference would be ideal.

She bit her lip, reading and rereading the message from Craig. He left no message. He didn't say to call him back. But he left his number, his lab number rather than his clinic. Did that mean to call him? Probably he was concerned that she was at work instead of resting. Or perhaps he just wondered about Sweetpea. Oh, what the heck? She dialed his lab number.

A woman answered. "Oh, Ms. Hill. He's in the lab, but he said if you called to patch you right through. Hang on, and I'll transfer you."

"Hi." His voice was calm and casual. She had the feeling that he was not alone. "I couldn't reach you at home. Mrs. Hill said you had left for work, despite my recommendation. When you hadn't reached there in a reasonable time, I was worried. Are you all right?"

She leaned back in the chair, smiling to herself. So he was worried about her? Was that professionally or personally? "I'm sorry, Craig, but there were things I had to do at work today. And I did go early to get Sweetpea. He's safely at home now. I am fine, but you were right about that shiner. It's full Technicolor."

"Just so you are all right."

"I am and, Craig? Thanks for last night. I enjoyed being with you." Lin grimaced. Did that make her appear needy and vulnerable? A single mother couldn't afford that appearance.

"Me too. I'll talk to you tonight, or maybe I'll see you? Okay?"

"Yeah, tonight," Lin said. No time to think about such things. She needed to get that information on Delia. She replaced the sunglasses and left her office. Passing Bess's desk, she said, "I'll be in the library a few minutes. While I'm gone, will you pull Delia's contract for this last book, please?"

She was surprised to run into Brad Benton in the corridor. He seemed just as surprised to see her. He stuffed his hands into his pants pockets and rocked back and forth nervously. "Ding dong, the wicked witch is dead," he said. He laughed nervously. "Oops, shouldn't let my feelings show, should I?" His features were sharp, with a narrow chin that was nearly split by a deep cleft. It made him appear almost sinister at times.

"How did you find out, Brad?" Lin asked.

"Why, the papers, of course."

"But it wasn't in the papers yet. Guess again," Lin challenged.

"Oh, you know the rumor mill. It grinds on and on. Oops, I think that was my telephone. Talk to you later. And sorry about that remark. It was tactless."

"And tasteless," Lin added. Right then she felt as if she could strike him. She hurried away before she said anything else. Moreover, she was sure his phone had not rung at all. At the library, she pulled *Contemporary Authors* from the shelf. Under Delia's name, she had given her mother's name as Althea Grainger and Robert Dorrs as her father.

She replaced the book on the shelf and returned to her office. Delia's contract was on her desk. She copied the social security number from it. Lin fished into her purse for her own credit cards to find the phone numbers. While her own were very limited in credit, she guessed that Delia would surely have a gold or platinum card with her income. She dialed the first 800 number.

"My name is Delia Dorrs, and I need to get a copy of the last six months of my charges, please."

"Your credit card number?"

"I'm sorry, but I'm at the office, and I left it at home," Lin said.

"For security purposes, what is your social security card number, please?"

Lin read the numbers slowly.

"And your mother's maiden name?"

"Althea Grainger."

"Yes, ma'am. That will be mailed to you."

"Oh, no!" Lin protested. Her mind was searching for a reason for haste. "I'm being audited. And the IRS man will be here any minute, and I have GOT to have those records. Have you ever had to face an audit without ALL your papers? I'm terrified. Can't you fax it to me?" She figured that most people would cringe at the mention of the tax collector.

"That's awfully irregular, ma'am," the assistant replied.

"Listen, maybe you'd better start a new precedent. They just might come after you! What's your name?"

The silence on the other end was deafening to Lin. She held her breath.

"Uh, I—I guess I can do this. What is the fax number?" The implied threat had paid off.

Lin gave her the number. "Will you send it instantly? Time is of the essence!"

When the woman agreed, Lin thanked her and hung up. She hurried to the communal fax machine which was in a closet-sized room on the west side of the building near the stairwell.

Lin paced nervously, pausing only to stare at the machine. *Ring, darn it, ring!*

Finally it rang, then hummed dramatically, as page after page rolled out and was deposited on the wire stand. At last, it stopped spewing Delia's records. Lin snatched them up and headed back to her office.

Bess was on her break. Good. Lin sat at her desk and sorted the pages. Sure enough—airlines, hotels, cabs— there would be plenty of evidence once she had deciphered it. Her phone rang.

It was Craig again. His voice was almost a whisper and edgy. "Lin, Trey wants to bring you in."

"What!" Lin felt as if her entire blood supply had instantly drained into her feet. "Why?"

"I think it would be best if you beat him to it and got your lawyer to come in with you. Don't talk to Trey without counsel."

"He's coming to my office?" Lin asked incredulously. "Why?" she asked again.

"I can't say. I'm putting my head on the block, calling you like this. But I didn't want him to come to your work. You know how it would look. Just get your lawyer and have him make arrangements to bring you in."

Frantically, Lin looked about her small office. She felt like a bird trapped in a cage. And the cat was closing in.

She had to get out of there. "When?"

"He and another deputy have already left; I don't know what time. Don't go home, Lin, you hear? You don't want him showing up with Jeffrey there, do you? Go to your lawyer's office. Tell him to negotiate a surrender for you."

Lin wiped her eyes. Dear, sweet Craig. She could have hugged him at that moment. The only lawyer she was familiar with was a divorce lawyer. "Why does he want me?"

"Lin, did you ever possess an editing trophy?"

"Yes, it's here on my desk. Why?"

"It's there? You have only one?"

"Yes, and I'm looking at it right now." She pulled it toward her, wondering what the big deal was all about. The polished brass plate said Top Editor, 1994. Lin felt her skin inch up her arms. Her trophy was for 1997. She turned it bottom up. Lin sucked in her breath. *Puede ser! It can't be!* There, scratched on the bottom, was Brad Benton's name. She felt icy cold. Her name was on the bottom of hers too.

Yesterday's conversation between Craig and Trey flashed into her mind. Craig had told Trey that Delia was killed with an odd-shaped object. And Trey had said that he could furnish that when the time came. He knew even then that it belonged to her. "Oh, God. Oh, no." Her breath came in gulps. *"¡Dios mio!* What am I going to do?"

Lin dropped the phone onto her desk. She quickly gathered the papers with Delia's travel expenses. They were her only hope now. To clear herself, she had to prove it was someone else, and she couldn't do it from a jail cell.

Craig's voice bellowed through the receiver, pleading with her. "Lin, Lin! Talk to me, Lin. I know what you're thinking, but don't! Trust me! Please, Lin, don't run!"

CHAPTER 10

Lin stuffed the papers into her purse and stepped to the door. Bess was still away from her desk, and no one was in the hall. Good. No one to see her leaving. She headed for the elevators in the reception area but suddenly thought what if Trey and his deputy were already on their way up? She might run into them at the elevators. Lin retraced her steps.

Terrible thoughts jumbled in her mind. The phone! She had not hung up the phone; what if Trey discovered that Craig had called her? He would be in terrible trouble, and one of them was enough! Had she destroyed his message? Bess had taken his first call; would she tell Trey if asked? No, not Bess. She would be puzzled, but she would not betray her. Lin replaced her receiver, snatched up the phone messages, and hurriedly returned to the library. She trotted toward the freight elevator at the back and pushed the call button.

Shifting back and forth on her feet, she silently pleaded, *Hurry, please hurry*. At last the down light went off, indicating that the elevator was approaching.

The overhead pager sounded. "Will Lin Hill please come to the reception area? Lin Hill, please come to the reception area."

They were here! Come on, come on. Quick, before they start to look for her! The metal doors slid open with a clank, and she lifted the wooden overhead gate by its rope. Hastily she stepped in as she heard her name paged again. Lin pulled down the gate and pushed the basement button. The elevator crept at a snail's pace until she thought she would die of terror. At last it bumped to a stop. Lin pulled open the gate, and looking neither to the right nor left, she hurried through the warehouse and off the loading dock.

What now? She was a fugitive on the run. She didn't know what to do or where to go to be safe from Trey's pursuit. *Think, Lin, think!* Trey would soon discover she had skipped. He will put out an APB on her, wasn't that the term—all points bulletin? *Who cares what the term is, Lin, run!* Her every instinct was telling her to get lost; it would be easy in a city this large. Her car? No, she must abandon it for now; her Beetle was so distinctive she'd be spotted in a second. Voices were yelling in her head, *¡Peligroso! ¡Vámonos! Dangerous! Let's go!* Jeffrey—what would he think of his mom? She had to talk to Mom. She had to get away. How?

She realized she couldn't use credit cards, whatever she did. That would leave a paper trail. Cash can't be traced. The bank! She needed to withdraw cash from the bank. Lin's shoes slapped the pavement as she rushed toward the bank. *It's okay to run*, she told herself. *In New York City, no one pays attention*. How much should she get? A thousand? Two thousand? *Sorry about your college fund, Jeffrey, but your mom is a fugitive and needs getaway money.* Enough cash to get her to Kentucky for starters. That's the first place Delia charged. Why else would she have been there? Surely the answer to this puzzle and to her own freedom was there.

How to get there, car rental? No, even if she used cash, they'd insist on a credit card for security. Plane? They want ID too. The bus! They don't care about ID, just the cash. But not the nearby terminal. That would be too obvious.

Lin realized that whether she used the automated teller machine or wrote a check, it was a paper trail. But that wouldn't tell them anything—only that she was on the run. That they would already know. She slipped into the bank and hastily wrote a check. "Nothing larger than 20s please," she said.

Although the teller looked at her suspiciously for writing for such a large amount and wearing her sunglasses inside the bank, Lin had the proper identification. There would be her picture on the surveillance now. But what would that get them?

Stuffing the cash into her purse, she headed for the restroom. There she removed the scarf from her hips and wrapped it carefully over and around her head, crossed it under her chin, then tied it at the back of her neck. She tucked every dark strand beneath the scarf. Then she divided up the money. Forty dollars in the billfold in plain sight. Another forty hidden in its secret compartment. The rest she spread as thinly as possible behind the torn lining of her purse. It didn't pay to show much money at a time. Replacing the glasses, she clutched the purse to her chest and hurried out of the bank. An unoccupied cab approached; she hailed it.

When it stopped, Lin jumped in. *Be calm*, she told herself. *Don't raise suspicions*. Instinct told her not to speak. She jotted an address near the bus terminal. She didn't want to give the driver the actual address. She could walk the few blocks. She handed him the note.

He looked in the rearview mirror at her. Raising his hand, he brushed his forefinger and thumb together. "Not until I see *la diñero, señorita*. Show me the money."

Lin fought the urge to tell him off. She pulled the two twenties from her purse and waved them, then jammed them back into her purse and snapped it shut.

"Okay, okay. I'm going."

Lin leaned back and sniffled. Was she doing the right thing, running like this? But how could she ever investigate Delia's expenses if she was in jail? She was not voluntarily going to be arrested, not until she had the proof she needed. But what had she done to Craig? His only vice was that he had tried to help her. And Jeffrey, dear Jeffrey. She couldn't hold back the tears any longer. Lin removed the sunglasses and dabbed her eyes with a tissue.

"Oh, man!" the driver said. "Your husband did that? Or your boyfriend?"

Lin blew her nose. "Huh?"

"Your shiner. *El ojo*, your eye? Your *esposo?*"

He obviously thought she spoke no English; Lin decided to play along. "*No, señor. El accidente.*"

"Oh, honey, don't protect him! He'll just do it again. You gotta get away. Don't go back there. There's a women's shelter I know. Hey, there's a cop. I can stop. You can tell him everything. *El policía. ¿Comprende?*"

Lin felt as if her heart would leap from her body. "*¡No, señor! ¡No el policía!*"

"Okay, okay, sweetheart. Have it your way. But you'll be sorry. You'll see."

He stopped at the appointed corner, and Lin looked at the meter. Six dollars. She handed him a twenty.

"*Gracias*, honey," he said and stuffed the bill into his pocket.

Lin shoved the glasses back on and gestured as he had, with her thumb and finger. "*¡Diñero!*" she said.

"Yeah, yeah. Never learn the language, but you sure learn the money, don't you sweetheart?" He handed her a ten.

"*¡Diñero!*" Lin shouted.

He handed her the other four and she jammed one back into his hand. "*Gracias*," she said and climbed out of the cab. If she weren't running and had more time, she'd take his name and registration and turn him in, but she couldn't afford to attract attention. He'd remember her, but he'd remember a Latino who couldn't speak English. The jerk!

When he was out of sight, Lin walked the two blocks to the bus terminal. She decided to keep up the little charade. "*Por favor, el autobús*," she said. "*Un boleto a* Louisville, Kentucky." When she reached into her purse, her hand struck something hard. It was Mom's cellular telephone; she had forgotten to return it last night. She pulled out three twenties and the three dollars she got in change from the cabby.

The ticket seller smiled at her. "It will take two of these and all of these."

She nodded. "*Si, gracias.*"

"Your luggage? Ah, *el bag*," the seller struggled for the right word as he drew a square in the air and pretended to lift it by the handle. "They need to load it in the cargo hold."

If she hadn't been so frightened, she'd probably have cracked up. *El bag?* Instead, Lin froze. No luggage. *Great way to call attention to yourself, Lin. The only one who travels without luggage!* "*El ladrón*," she replied. A thief was the best she could come up with at the moment.

"Aw, too bad. Will someone meet you there?"

"*Sí, señor, la madre mía.*"

"Gate two. *El portón dos*, got it?"

Lin took the ticket. "*Sí, gracias.*"

She stopped off in the restroom. Lin dialed the Hills on the cellular phone. "Mom?"

"Oh, Mrs. McNeil! How nice of you to call," Mrs. Hill said.

"There's someone there?"

"Yes, Mrs. McNeil, Sunday brunch sounds lovely."

"Trey's men?"

"Yes, I can bring a casserole."

Lin sniffled. "Mom, take care of Jeffrey. I have a lead on the killer, and I won't turn myself in until I follow it through. I love y'all. I'll call when I get there."

"Oh, I don't think that's a good idea, Mrs. McNeil. That doesn't go very well with pumpkin soup, but I'll think of something."

Lin punched the "end call" button. Mom probably thinks they will bug her phone or keep someone watching. Or perhaps she was telling her that following her lead was a bad idea. She hoped the cellular phone held out.

On the bus, Lin sat by a window on her shiner side. That way, she could remove the glasses and examine the expenses more closely. The credit card company included miniature copies of the charges. There were taxi rides, hotels, meals, even Xerox charges; Delia was very meticulous.

Lin planned to retrace Delia's visit. Therein lies the answer; she was sure of it. Satisfied that she knew where to begin, Lin turned her head to watch the scenery. Anything to keep her mind off home and Jeffrey and the Hills and Craig. She had let them down, all of them. She may even have cost Craig his job.

She had hurt her family, but they would forgive her. But what about Craig? She realized she cared what he thought more than she should. She had known him only three days, yet she trusted him despite her misgivings. After Gerald, she had promised herself that she would never be so trusting and vulnerable again. She had a lot of explaining and apologizing to do, but the first step was to find Delia's killer. She could apologize better when there were no prison bars between them.

Lin considered, maybe she shouldn't have run off; she should have stayed there and shown Trey the trophy with Brad's name. Oh, no! He would have thought she did it just to cover up. But if her trophy was found at Delia's, and Brad's was in her office, why hadn't Brad noticed his missing?

Had Brad placed his own trophy there, knowing that eventually she would be blamed for the switch? How had he found out about Delia, and why had he been so nervous?

If she had made the wrong assumptions, she'd know it soon enough. A chill passed through her. What if Delia's killer found her before she found the killer? After all, someone had used her trophy as the weapon. Trey had to be desperate to believe she did it. What fool would carry her own trophy with her name emblazoned on it, kill someone with it, then leave it behind? Someone had set her up to look like the murderer. Who?

CHAPTER 11

Once Lin reached
Louisville, she bought a canvas backpack, a change of
clothes, and necessities. Trey would check all the chain
motels and hotels. Their computer hookups could
provide instant information about guests anywhere in the
world. She didn't intend to make it easy on him.

Lin stuffed the purchases into the backpack. Satisfied
that she looked more like a legitimate traveler, she
located an independent motel on the outskirts of town
in the Yellow Pages and called a cab.

Her room was cramped with its plain furnishings. The
drapes didn't quite meet to shut out the light, and soon
the sun cut a bright slice through the dreary little room.
It reminded her of all the movies of fugitives on the run.
All it needed was a leaky, noisy window air conditioner.

After changing into jeans and sweatshirt, she pulled
the motel stationery and pen from the desk and retrieved

the Yellow Pages from the bedside drawer. Lin jotted down the addresses and numbers of the cab company and library. Lin thought her first stop should be the cab company. She needed to find out Delia's destinations. Her cab bill was huge and in a lump sum. There was no way to tell if she made many small stops or one long trip. Lin gave the cab dispatcher the corner address a block away. She didn't want to be seen by the cabby leaving the motel or her room.

"To your dispatcher's office," she told him.

"I can patch you through right here, if you need to talk to her, ma'am," he said.

She smiled. "Thank you, but no; I need to speak to the dispatcher in person."

She paid him and added a 15 percent tip because he was polite; it reminded her of her native Texas more than her adopted home. In the office, she spoke to the young woman between dispatches. "I need to speak to the driver who took this call. It's dated 3:30 P.M., November 11th."

"Are you a detective? Is there something wrong?" the young woman wanted to know.

"No, but it's a matter of life and death."

The woman flipped through her book to November 11 of the previous year. With her finger she traced down the page. "Here, yeah. Tiny Green took the call. Pick up at the Downtown Marriott and drove her to—that's odd. There's no destination here. He checked out, said he was off call for the rest of the day. He owns his own cab, so maybe she hired him to drive all day." The woman looked at Lin long and hard, then pushed the button on her mike. "Tiny, do you have a passenger? Over."

"Negative, Joyce. Over."

"Return to the barn immediately. Over."

"Is something wrong? Over."

"Negative, Tiny. A lady here needs to talk to you. 10-4." She turned to Lin. "You can stay here in the cage until he comes if you want."

Tiny arrived shortly. He was just the opposite of his name. He looked as if he weighed at least 300, and Lin marveled that he fit behind the wheel at all. He looked anxious.

"Please," Lin said, "back on November 11th you picked up a woman from the Marriott. Middle-aged, platinum blond, and—"

Tiny nodded. "Who could forget her? Very stuck-up. But she didn't mind spreading the dough. She told me to keep the meter running and wait. She was in that place for two hours, and she didn't even blink when I billed her—just stuck it on a gold card. I ran it through right away to be sure it was okay; I couldn't afford to be out that much dough. I took her lots of places that day, but I never saw her again."

Lin asked, "Do you remember the destinations or anything about that day?"

"You're kidding! No cabby is going to forget hitting the passenger lottery. I remember every place we went. And if memory fails, I got it in my personal log book."

"Would you take me to the first place?" Lin asked.

Tiny's eyes sparkled. "You want to hire me to retrace her trips?"

Lin shook her head. "I don't have her kind of money, Tiny. But I am willing to pay you for information. It's terribly important."

"It's a matter of life and death, she said," Joyce told him.

"My log book's in the cab. Come on, lady. Let's go," Tiny said.

Tiny handed his log book over the seat to Lin. "Right there. You'll see everywhere she went. The nursing home, the library, newspaper, the police station, then a residence before going back to the hotel. She didn't stay long at the police station, though—just came tearing out of there and gave me that last address to go to. I waited a long time there too."

"A nursing home?" Lin asked. "That was her first stop, and she stayed there a long time?" She felt as if her hopes had just dashed against the rocks. She was wishing for a private residence, not some place that housed anywhere from ten to a hundred or so. How would she find the right source? She had an idea. "Tiny, stop off at a florist, please. I want to pick up a plant."

Tiny pulled in front of a small florist. He grinned at her. "For you, I'll stop the meter running, okay?"

Lin thanked him and dashed inside. She spotted a pink azalea plant, quickly paid for it, and left. Tiny pulled in front of the nursing home. "You sure you don't want me to wait?"

"No, but tell you what. I'll request you when I call for a cab, and if you're not already occupied, it's a deal, okay?"

Lin paid him and added $40 for the information; she hoped it was worth it. She walked through the automatic doors of the nursing home. Like a welcome beacon, a sign announced that all visitors must sign in. The information desk was also the central phone system, so the woman was occupied answering and rerouting phone calls. Lin held her breath as she set down the plant and picked up the attached pen. She smiled at the woman, who just nodded and turned away. The guest book asked the name of the guests and the resident they would visit, the date, and the time.

Cautiously Lin turned the pages back to November 11. There was Delia's hastily scrawled name. The resident's name was Annie Sue Needham. Beneath that was another resident's name, Abigail Jones Dyer. On the current page, Lin signed her name as Esperanza Mendoza and entered Abigail's name. "What room is Ms. Needham in?" Lin asked.

The woman smiled at her. "Oh, she will be so thrilled with that azalea. She just loves flowers. She doesn't get many visitors. Room 132, down that hall there, but she's out on the patio this morning, enjoying the nice sunny day." She pointed. "Straight through those glass doors."

Lin thanked her and picked up the azalea. "I—I haven't seen her in a long time. Does she look the same?"

"Oh, same as ever, honey. Sweet-faced and busy with her handiwork, like always. It's just her poor old legs have given out on her."

On the patio, Lin saw a dozen men and women; some playing cards, some nodding off. She spotted a woman in a wheelchair off to the side, crocheting. "Miss Needham?" Lin asked.

The woman looked up and over her half-glasses at Lin. "Yes? Do I know you? Oh, my, is that beautiful flower for me?"

"Yes, ma'am, it is. We don't know each other, but we have a mutual acquaintance. Delia Dorrs." Lin set the plant down next to the woman's chair and pulled up a lawn chair for herself.

"Delia Dorrs? Delia Dorrs. No, I don't believe so."

"A woman, tall, blond, who came to see you last November. She asked you a lot of questions and stayed two or three hours, I think."

Ms. Needham put down her handwork. "Oh, my yes! Was that her name? I forget sometimes."

"But you remember what she wanted to know, don't you?"

"Oh my, yes. Tragic, simply tragic, I say. No need to bring up all that pain and suffering again."

"I wouldn't, ma'am," Lin persisted, "except that it is so important. It is a matter of life and death."

"Death," the woman repeated. "That's what it was all about. Death. Too many, yes, too many."

"Please?" Lin repeated.

"It was a long time ago, mind you. Bobby Symms was barely 20 at the time. And he just flat murdered his poor mama and daddy—bludgeoned them to death, he did. And him already married and the father of two little children. Just tragic," she said. "He took what little valuables they had and ran off, and his poor little wife was so distraught over the disgrace that she killed herself two years later—left those poor little children orphans. Oh my, yes."

"You say it was a long time ago. How long?" Lin asked.

"Well, let's see now. It must be 35, 40 years ago. Uh-huh. More like 40, I think. It was 1956. Does that make it 40? What year is this?"

"Do the children live here still?" Lin wanted to know.

"Oh, I don't think so. They got adopted out. Everyone wanted the little things, including me. But I was single. And you know they didn't give children to single people in those days, especially a single woman."

"No, ma'am," Lin agreed. "Did they get adopted together?"

"No, I don't think so. Cutest little babies you ever saw. Oh, how I'd love to see them now. I was their auntie, you know. Actually, great auntie. How Bobby could do that I don't know. He just left his poor mama and daddy dead in the living room in that cold, cold house. The police never found him. But his Maker knows where he is. He'll pay for bringing so much pain, yes sir."

"Yes, ma'am," Lin said. "I'm sure he will. Thank you, and enjoy the plant with my gratitude." Lin was aware that her own soft Texas twang had returned with her Southern manners. Her parents taught her to always say *ma'am* and *sir* to older people, a habit she had quickly lost in New York.

"Well, aren't you sweet? Too sweet to be thinking about that awful past," Miss Needham said.

Lin went to the main lobby to call a cab, but she saw one in front. Lin went out and opened the door. The large silhouette at the wheel made her smile. "Tiny? You waited?"

He laughed heartily. "It's slow today, and you seem like a nice lady. Where to?"

"To the library, Tiny. The central library, I suppose. It's probably the one with microfiche of old newspapers, isn't it?"

Tiny laughed. "I wouldn't know. I have enough trouble with today's news, let alone digging into the old stuff. But I reckon you're right. It is the biggest one."

He let her out at the front entrance. "Good luck, ma'am. I reckon I best get back on the road again."

Lin opened her purse to pay him.

He waved her off. "Your tip earned you this trip, ma'am." He drove off.

Inside, the librarian at the front desk directed her to the microfiche and film department. There, Lin filled in the request form and handed it to the research librarian. The woman returned with the appropriate film spools, and Lin loaded a machine. Surely such a bloody story would have made the front page. Perhaps she could concentrate on front pages. She only hoped that Miss Needham's memory was sharp and that she was close to the correct year. She had said the house was cold. Perhaps it was still winter.

Lin spent the better part of the day searching for the appropriate article. She found it on the front page of the February 1956 newspapers. There were photos of Bobby Symms, of his parents, Reverend and Mrs. Stegner Symms, and of Bobby's wife and his two small children, a toddler boy and an infant girl. Reverend Symms: was that the reason for the title, *Gory Alleluia?* Lin read through subsequent papers, but the stories got smaller and far between as Bobby's whereabouts were never discovered.

Lin asked for the 1958 spool to read about Amy Symms, the distraught wife who killed herself. On a hunch, she started with the February papers; sometimes distressed people get more agitated on anniversaries. She was right. That poor girl and those poor little children. Four lives gone because of Bobby Symms—his parents, his wife, and now Delia. Two more lives perhaps ruined; what about those children? They would be, according to these accounts, perhaps forty-three and forty-five years old now, but who adopted them? What were their names now? There was something vaguely familiar about Bobby's face. She felt as if she had seen it many times.

CHAPTER
12

Lin took the spools to the librarian. "Condensed copies of the whole pages of these issues I've marked with the sticky notes," she said. "And I'd like to get blowups of the photos." When the librarian returned with the copies, Lin asked, "Do you have a public fax machine?"

"It's at the front; 15 cents a page. And these copies are 25 cents each," she replied.

Lin took her copies to the front desk. She pulled Craig's business card from her wallet. But would he be willing to help her after she had run? There was but one way to find out. Mom's cellular phone was still well charged, and since Mom used nationwide service, it would still carry the assigned area code and not betray her location.

Lin dialed Craig's lab. A woman answered.

"Por favor, el doctor. La emergencia," Lin said, hoping

that the Spanish would clue Craig that it was she.

She was right; he answered instantly. *"Hola,"* he answered loudly. In almost a whisper, he said, "Lin? Where are you?"

Lin ignored his question so as not to compromise his position with Trey any more than she already had. "I have a lead. And I think I know who did it. I want to fax you some photos. Can you put them in your magical aging machine and add forty to forty-three years? Please?"

"Lin—" She heard him let his breath out in a surrendering sigh. "You have the number?"

"Yes, and I'll owe you big-time."

"Big-time enough to realize that I care what happens to you? Big enough so that you will trust me?" he asked.

Tears splashed onto her cheeks. "Craig, I—*lo siento*. I'm sorry. Stand by for the faxes." She pushed the "end call" button.

Lin counted out the sheets. Fifteen. She gave the librarian $2.25 and Craig's fax number. Tomorrow she would call him. By that time he should have a good idea what Bobby Symms looks like today. And having photos of the two parents, he should be able to do an approximate look on the two children. If she was right, the toddler would bear a striking resemblance to Brad Benton.

Did Delia track her story back to him? Why else would Brad have murdered Delia except to keep the scandal of his father away from his door? With what she had found out, surely that would put Trey on the right track and get him off hers.

With the entire fax and information in Craig's capable hands, Lin called the cab dispatcher and requested that she page Tiny if he was available. While she waited, she reread the articles, hoping that Delia's train of thought in her research would show. Would the death of the Reverend Symms be enough for Delia to name her book *Gory Alleluia*? It did seem like a reach; Delia's titles were always to the heart of the information. The Reverend Symms was a player, but not the main player in this drama. The articles said that the primary detective on the Symms murders was a Joseph Leopold.

In less than twenty minutes, Tiny arrived. "To the police station?" he asked in his slow drawl. "I figure you are still following the lady's tracks. And that was where she went next."

As little as Lin wanted to be in the vicinity of a police station or anyone connected with it, Detective Leopold seemed like the next logical step. On the way, she reviewed Delia's later credit charges. From Kentucky, Delia went to Toledo, Ohio. There she rented a car. There were charges for meals and gasoline, though, that might be more direct clues. Lin needed a map of Ohio. What connection did Ohio have to Bobby Symms? Or to Brad Benton, for that matter?

Lin wondered if maybe she was barking up the wrong family tree. And if she was, she would remain the best suspect in Trey's mind.

Tiny pulled to a stop in front of the central police station. "I'm gonna wait right over there, but I'll watch the door for you to come out. I don't think you'll stay long, because the lady didn't."

Lin thanked him and stood hesitantly, looking at the doors into the station. *Get real, Lin. You're hardly on the FBI's Ten Most Wanted list*, she told herself. *Don't be such a little scared chicken.*

She felt she was calling more attention to herself by standing there than by doing what she came to do. She went to the desk sergeant. "May I speak to Detective Joseph Leopold?" she asked.

"Detective Leopold retired three years ago, but since he never liked fishing or golf, you'll probably find him at home in his wood shop if you want him personally. He's in the book. Oh, right. This is Tuesday. That's the night he goes to his daughter's. Or maybe it's poker night." The sergeant said, "If it's to place a complaint, any of the detectives can take that, ma'am. Straight through that door."

"Complaint?" Lin echoed.

"Assault, maybe. This is about that shiner, isn't it?"

Lin backed up as her hand automatically reached for her eye. "No! This was an accident. I hit a door."

"Uh-huh." His voice dripped with doubt.

"I—I wanted to speak with Detective Leopold about one of his old cases," Lin said. "I'll try his home as you suggested."

"This about the Symms case?"

Lin's mouth flew open in surprise. She backed another step.

He grinned. "Just a wild guess, ma'am. That's been a real popular case for the last six months for some weird reason. Fact is, just got a request to wire some photographs regarding that case. Of course, there's no time limit on murder."

The desk phone rang, and he answered. While he was on the phone, Lin hurried out. She signaled Tiny as she emerged from the building, and he pulled the cab to the curb.

Lin glanced at her watch. "It's after 6, Tiny. I guess I'd better return to—I'd better call it a day. You too?" She had almost given up the name of the motel.

"Good idea, ma'am. Call me direct," Tiny said. He handed her a card. "That's the number. When you're ready to start tracking tomorrow, I'm your man."

She gave Tiny the address of the intersection two blocks from the motel, and he drove her there. She paid him for the additional rides and waited until he had driven off before walking back to the motel. Lin stopped at the little cafe next door and got a turkey sandwich and salad to go. She felt more comfortable eating in her room, away from staring eyes.

Lin turned on the television just for the noise factor. She had never felt so lonely in her life. She longed to be with her sweet Jeffrey. She craved the supporting hugs from the Hills. And despite herself, she yearned for the sight of Craig's probing blue eyes, his comforting smile, and his willing arms. By sharing her finding on the Symms case with him, she had invested more trust in him than she had dared with any man in years; she could only hope that she was right.

Lin did her best to sleep; her body was so bone-tired that she needed it badly. But her mind wouldn't shut down. She was haunted with visions of Delia and of herself running, running, running, with the scene never changing. She dreamed she was standing before closed doors. There was a smiling master of ceremonies. "Lin Hill, behind one door is the murderer you seek. Behind another is Lieutenant Trey, waiting to take you in. And behind the third door is the happily-ever-after life you seek. Which door do you choose?"

Lin awakened crying. She spent the rest of the night sitting in the chair, staring at the sliver of moonlight that cut through the room. At last, morning came. She redressed and went to the cafe for coffee and a newspaper. Returning to her room, she looked up Joseph Leopold's telephone number. She read the newspaper until she considered it a decent hour of the morning to phone him for an appointment. Then she called Tiny.

As they drove across town, Lin was only vaguely aware of the scenery. She was wondering who had requested the photographs and why. Had Craig told Lieutenant Trey?

Tiny pulled in front of a white-trimmed colonial-style house. The yard was neatly cut, and flowers lined the walk. The shrill sound of an electric saw invaded Lin's ears as she exited the taxi. It seemed to be coming from behind the house. Before she closed the taxi door, she asked Tiny, "Don't you want to leave?"

"I think I'll just turn off the meter and take a little snooze while you're in there, ma'am," he said. "I'll be right here, waiting for you."

Lin followed the noise up the driveway to a double garage at the rear of the house. The doors were opened, and a gray-haired man was hunkered over a worktable, concentrating on his task. Lin waited until he shut off the saw so that she could be heard. "Detective Leopold?" she asked.

He looked up and, as he did, slid his protective goggles to the top of his head. "Just plain old Mister, now. But call me Joseph. What can I do for you, young lady?"

"You worked the Symms murders and suicide?" Lin asked.

He removed the goggles and nodded. "Come around to the patio. I'm ready for a juice break. Will you join me?" He grasped the sweating pitcher and poured two glasses. "Have a seat. And your name is—?"

Lin introduced herself.

Joseph sat down and sipped his cranberry juice. "And you are interested in that old case because—?"

"I am an editor, and one of my authors wrote a book about that case. She, er, she died before completing it. I'm following through on it, verifying facts and so forth."

"Oh, that blond woman, Delia Dorrs, wasn't it? She came to see me about six months ago. And she's dead?

She looked pretty healthy, but I guess you never know, do you?"

Lin shook her head. "No, I guess you don't. Sir, I want to know, were you able to tell her things about the case that weren't in the newspapers? Anything that might help identify Bobby Symms?"

Joseph stared off into space a minute, then closed his eyes. "Oh, my, Bobby Randall Symms. He haunts me in my dreams." He took a deep breath and turned toward Lin. "I never wanted to close a case more in my life than that one. I hated to retire with it hanging over my head. It was a brutal scene—just brutal. Sent the city into an uproar. Of course, one thing never came out in the papers—we try to keep a few things out, just to have something that only the killer knows for sure. That way, when we finally catch him, it's a way of double-checking, weeding out those weird ones that come in to confess to every crime from the Lindbergh kidnapping to the sinking of the *Titanic*."

He took another sip before continuing. "Oh, we know it was the boy—his bloody prints were everywhere. And they were all over the murder weapon—a fireplace poker. He didn't make any attempt to cover up. Just disappeared. The parents were strong disciplinarians, I discovered. There was apparently a lot of abuse as he was growing up, but friends and the congregation just turned their heads the other way back then. There wasn't a law like today that says if you know of such abuse and don't report it, you can be charged. It wasn't a major religion, just a self-contained one with Symms owning the church building and everything. I don't know; today we'd probably call it a cult, you know? There was a plaque hanging in the living room of the parsonage with that quote, 'Spare the rod and spoil the child.' Bobby Symms had written over it in blood. It said, 'Vengeance is mine, sayeth the Lord.'

"All things considered, Bobby might have gotten off with a temporary insanity plea or something. He worked as a janitor at his father's church, which must have been a big letdown for his father. Reverend Symms had trained the boy up in the church; I suppose he expected him to take over after he passed on. But Bobby stole stuff—the silver communion cup and plate, his mother's rings, and other valuables. They weren't poor, understand. It was plain cold-blooded murder; he must have caught them completely unaware. Bobby ran off after the murders, deserting his wife and kids. I have wondered whatever happened to those sweet little children."

Lin nodded sympathetically. She didn't tell him that she thought that one of those sweet little children was a murderer too. Unless Bobby had continued his own life of crime. "Do you know what connection to Ohio there was?"

He raised an eyebrow. "Ohio? That's a new one on me. Why?"

"Oh, nothing, really. It may have no bearing on the case at all," Lin said. "Thank you, Joseph. You've been a big help."

"That case still bugs me, you know? If you ever come across something that might help clear it up, will you be kind enough to let me know?" he asked. He shook her hand. "Good-bye, and good luck, Ms. Hill."

Tiny roused when Lin opened the cab door. "Tiny, was there anyplace else that Miss Dorrs went that day?"

"No, ma'am, just back to the hotel. She was in the back, pecking away on one of those little laptop computers, you know, with just two fingers, and she went straight back to the hotel. You look plumb worn-out. Bet you didn't eat anything for breakfast either, did you? Most important meal of the day too."

"I suppose I didn't, Tiny. I forgot. I still have much to do yet." Something her father used to say flashed into her

memory: "I got miles to go and rows to hoe." Her heart
fairly ached for friends and family right now. She just
wanted to hear Jeffrey's voice, to tell him she loved him.
Mom had warned her not to call, though. Lin sighed
wearily. "Back to the library, Tiny."

On the way, she pulled out the cellular phone and
dialed Craig's lab. Surely he would have the faces in the
photographs redone by now. *"El doctor, por favor,"* Lin said
when the woman answered.

The woman hesitated. "Dr. Gleason is—uh, is not
going to be here for an indefinite period. May I relay
a message to him?"

Lin pushed the "end" button. The words reverberated in
her brain. Not going to be here for an indefinite period?
He's been suspended for helping her! What had she done?
Craig was the one person in a position to help her, and
she had caused him to be suspended, maybe even to lose
the job he loved. What if he was accused of aiding and
abetting, or conspiracy? Whatever, it was all her fault, and
she must clear him. To do that, she had to clear herself.

CHAPTER 13

At the library, Lin asked about Ohio phone directories. "I don't know the city or town."

"We have a computer available for at least the next hour," the librarian told her. "If no one requests it, you can use it longer."

Lin signed the request sheet. "The directories are on a computer now?"

The librarian motioned for Lin to follow her. "Let me show you. Click here where it says *search*. It gives you a choice of the *White* or *Yellow Pages*. Now it seeks all the information you already know. Just fill in the blanks and click *enter*. It will do the rest."

When she had left, Lin took a deep breath. She looked at the charge list. Reliable Rentals, Toledo, Ohio. That's probably where she should start. She clicked on *enter*, and the phone number and address of the auto rental appeared on the screen.

Lin pulled out her cellular and dialed the number. "This is Delia Dorrs, and I rented a Monte Carlo from you three days in November of last year. I need to know the number of miles that I clocked."

Drumming her fingers on the desk, she waited while the accountant pulled the files. "That was a total of 275 miles," the woman told her.

Lin reviewed the charges. Delia had stayed in a hotel in downtown Toledo, three nights' charges. That had to mean that she was commuting daily. If she divided the mileage by six, that would give her about 48 to 49 miles. If she drew a circle using Toledo as a center point, she might check every direction on the outskirts of that circle.

Clicking on *search* again, Lin typed in "Ohio+map." When it appeared, Lin ordered a printout. She checked the legend for the scale and drew a rough circle. "Now what?" she asked herself. "Pick a direction, any direction?"

She startled at the tap on her shoulder. "I'm sorry," the librarian said. "Your hour is up, and the computer is reserved for the next two hours."

"But I'm just starting to make headway here," Lin said.

"If you don't mind paying for computer time, there is a Computeria about five blocks north of here," the librarian suggested. "You rent time on a computer. If you hurry, you can beat the lunch crowd. It fills up pretty fast when the office workers start taking breaks." She wrote down the address. "Go out the front door and turn right."

Lin thanked her and gathered her papers. When she had gone about five blocks, she saw the sign and quickened her pace.

The manager greeted her at the door. "It's by the hour, plus any printouts."

Lin spread her papers in front of her. She saw that Delia had eaten at a Randallston Inn twice and made purchases at Randallston Gift Shop. She studied her map. There was no Randallston on it, inside or outside her circle.

Lin stared at the charge. Randallston Gift Shop. Randallston Inn. There had to be a Randallston, whether or not it was on the map. She typed in Randallston+Ohio.

A brightly colored home page appeared. "Welcome to the beautiful campus of Randallston, a religious compound less than an hour away from downtown Toledo."

As she read, her pulse quickened. "Visit Randallston Inn, adjacent to the Randallston Golden Hours home for the retired. Insist that your local stations carry our syndicated worship hours. Enroll in our Randallston Bible College and worship at the Cathedral of the Avenging Angel with the Reverend Robert Randall." She clicked on the button next to the Reverend Randall's name. Instantly, an image of the man appeared. His snow-colored hair curled about his ears and fell to his shoulders. He wore a flowing white beard. His biography listed his credentials. It said he had a doctorate in divinity, and he had set up a charitable foundation that had collected millions for the benefit of the helpless and for scholarships for needy students.

Lin bit her lip, studying the pages. What about this attracted Delia? Where there was money, there was power. Where there was power, there was the potential for abuse. Had Delia uncovered abuse of power, a cult-like atmosphere, or what? And what did it have to do with Bobby Symms?

Something about the combination of the minister's name and that of his church struck a familiar chord. She tried to remember Detective Joseph Leopold's words: "Bobby Randall Symms—he haunts me in my dreams."

Lin had read about abused children like Bobby. Some protected themselves by shutting down all feelings or developing multiple personalities. Some adopted the role of victim all their lives. And some identified with the abuser and his power and emulated him. Is it possible that Bobby Randall Symms was one of the latter, and he became like his father? All this time, he was hiding in plain sight, and no one was the wiser until Delia found him. Lin was sure that beneath that flowing white beard was a deeply ridged cleft chin.

It was all coming very clear to her. Delia had put two and two together, but she came up with five! And it got her killed. She must've confronted Brad with her findings, and he determined to kill her to keep his secret. He no doubt killed Dottie too, because as secretary she was privy to what Delia knew.

Lin clicked on *print* and ordered three copies each of every page about the Reverend Robert Randall, aka Bobby Randall Symms. She gathered her papers and took them to the checkout desk.

"You must've had very good luck today," the manager said. "You've been at it five hours."

"Gosh," Lin said, "I guess time flies when you're having fun, huh? Mind if I stay inside until my cab arrives?"

She called the dispatcher and asked for Tiny.

Lin stuffed the papers into her purse and hugged her purse to her. What a find! She felt as if she had out-detected Sherlock Holmes himself. Surely with this information, she could convince Lieutenant Trey that it was Brad who had killed Delia and had set her up as the murderer. And surely he would see that Craig remained a medical examiner, despite his helping her. After all, what crime is there in helping an innocent person?

While she waited, she pulled out the cellular and

dialed Craig's pager number. Even if he wasn't at the lab or the clinic, surely he kept his pager with him. Would he recognize the number and return the call? He was probably so disgusted with her by now that he would not return the call even if he did recognize it.

The battery indicator beeped. That was the last of the charge. Blast it, anyway. A horn sounded, and Lin looked up to see Tiny's taxi. She scooted out the door and climbed in. "Tiny, do you know of a store that sells cellular phone accessories? I need to get a re-charge plug."

Tiny pulled into the parking lot of a strip mall.

Lin hurried into a Radio Shack and returned with her purchase. An overnight charge ought to get the cellular back on line, she figured. The sun was disappearing quickly. "Drive on to the Wilton Motel, Tiny. Stop at the office, please."

She paid Tiny and entered the manager's office. There she purchased a stamp and got an envelope. Lin addressed it to Joseph Leopold and folded a set of the printouts on Reverend Randall into it. She added the stamp and tossed it into the outgoing basket.

Outside the door, she paused, looking down the long stretch of rooms. The bushes near each door took on ominous shapes.

Lin froze in place as a movement caught her eye. A shadow near her door moved. It parted from the other shadows and became more distinct. She urged her feet to run, but they were rooted to the ground. It was a man, and he was swiftly approaching her.

CHAPTER 14

Lin backed up slowly. "I see you! Don't come any closer! I have a weapon; I'll scream!" She felt her adrenaline kick in. *What weapon?* her mind was screaming. A key to the eye if necessary? Maybe swing her purse like a bolo? Even with the cellular phone in it, it wasn't heavy enough. *Think, Lin, think. What did your self-defense class teach you?* Kick and scream and gouge the eyes. If she had to, she knew she could run, but she wasn't sure she could outrun whoever it was waiting for her in the dark. Who? Brad? Bobby Symms? How did they find her? A stranger? She took another step back. "I'm warning you! Don't come any closer."

"Lin? *¡Hola!*"

It was as if every bit of her adrenaline poured from her eyes in tears as she breathed his name, "Craig!" Her shoulders quaked as she ran toward him, sobbing with relief. She leaped into his outstretched arms. "When I called and they said you were off indefinitely, I thought they had suspended you. And then I called the clinic and it was closed and you didn't respond on your pager and, oh, Craig, I am so sorry."

"Shh, shh. It 's going to be all right, *querida*," he said, stroking her hair. "I should be angry with you, but I am too relieved at seeing you."

"I didn't mean to get you in trouble, Craig. What have I done?" Lin fished for a tissue in her purse. She sniffled and dabbed at her eyes, taking a hiccuping breath. She looked at him intensely. Had he just called her *querida*? Darling? "You—you aren't angry? How did you find me? I used the cellular phone so that you wouldn't have even the area code. I thought I was being so clever."

"Elementary, dear Watson," he said, flicking a tear off her cheek. "Elementary. If the newspaper clippings hadn't clued me in, the library fax number across the top of every page you sent would have. You make a terrible fugitive, *mi amor.*"

Lin felt as if her head were spinning. First *querida* and now *mi amor*, my love? Such tender words for someone who caused him so much trouble. "All right, so I'm not so clever as to hide the city, but how did you track me to this motel? I deliberately avoided the chains with their computer hook-ups."

He grinned at her. "The Yellow Pages, a fistful of quarters, and dogged determination. I called them all. You would pick one that begins with a W." He took her hand. "Come with me; first, I'm going to feed you well. I have the distinct feeling that you have neglected yourself. Then I have a few things to show you."

"The pictures? You aged them? Let me see, oh, please." Lin tugged at his hand.

"Oh, no," Craig said. "You have caused me a lot of lost sleep. So you will wait until after dinner. That's my revenge."

He nodded toward a car. "That black sedan is my rental." He opened the passenger-side door. "The faxes you sent didn't give clear enough features for me to work with. I had the police here send me their files direct via computer."

Lin got in and snapped her seat belt. She followed him with her eyes as he walked around the front of the car and opened the driver-side door.

He slid in and glanced over, grinning at her. "What?"

Lin hadn't realized she was smiling until he said that. "I'm so glad you are here."

He pulled her toward him and to her surprise kissed her full on the lips, briefly at first, then a sweet, lingering kiss.

Lin swept her arms around his neck and responded with more enthusiasm that she had anticipated. She leaned back and took a deep breath. She could feel her heart thumping in her chest. "I could get used to that," she said.

"Good," he told her. "I was hoping you'd say that." He started the motor and shifted to drive. "When did you last eat?"

Lin shook her head. "I think last night. I'm all right, though." Suddenly she felt ravenous.

Craig drove to a seafood restaurant. "Hope this is okay," he teased. "I am vaguely uncomfortable eating red meat in a horse-racing city."

Lin laughed. "I definitely missed you and your sense of humor, Doc." When they were seated, Lin ordered baked fish, carrots, and green peas. When the waiter left to turn in their order, she said, "I followed Delia's movements here, Craig, and I think that—"

He shook his head. "Not now, Lin. There's plenty of time for that after dinner. You should just relax and enjoy the ambiance. That's what I want to do. I worked on those photos, arranged for a leave of absence in case this took longer, bought our plane tickets, and haven't had any sleep except on the plane, so I'm whipped."

He did look tired, and she immediately regretted that she'd been so wrapped up in her own thoughts that she hadn't noticed. *"Our* tickets?" Lin asked.

"I didn't exactly come here to say hello, Lin. I came to take you home. Jeffrey misses you. The Hills miss you." He shrugged. "And I—"

He let his words fade, but Lin understood. She unfolded her napkin and placed it in her lap. Home. Even if it meant facing Trey, home sounded wonderful.

When the plates arrived, Lin said, "Craig, I was never so delighted in my life as when I saw you. I will never misjudge or mistrust you again, I promise."

He reached across the table to take her hand. "How could you not think I would come? Haven't I been right there for you all through this?"

She squeezed his hand. "You have, but I can't for the life of me understand why after the way I have reacted."

He laughed. "To tell you the truth, I wasn't sure why either, until I saw you poised and ready to defend yourself in the parking lot. Then my own words came flying back at me: 'intelligent, stable, and has a sense of who she is . . .'"

She remembered his description of "the right one" and finished it. "'Not afraid of family commitment, someone to love and who'll love me.'" *Oh, yes!*

He leaned back in his chair and looked at her with those probing blue eyes. "I think we'll have to give a couple of those some time, but that's okay. As I said, I'm patient." He smiled that heart-melting smile.

She giggled. "Especially stable. You must think I am some kind of a nut, running off like that. I hated myself for fleeing, but I know that I did the right thing. I really feel I have some answers now to show to Lieutenant Trey, to prove to him that I didn't do it."

When they had eaten, the waiter brought the dessert tray, and Lin declined. "Life is sweet enough." Sweet to think that this great guy could love her, and frightening to think she might have blown it with her immature actions.

"Just the check, please," Craig told the waiter. When he had left, Craig said, "Trey has grudgingly admitted that your trophy was a plant, Lin. If you had just waited around a bit, you'd have seen that you were quickly cleared. Bess, of course, hesitantly admitted that you left early the day the victim was apparently held in bonds. That looked bad until Mrs. Hill remembered about the fiesta you threw. Trey's assistant found your grocery receipt on the kitchen counter and it was dated and timed. He spoke with the grocer who told them he had personally checked you out. All your time was accounted for, Lin. You shouldn't have panicked, *querida*."

Lin agreed. "I know, yet I might not have found the murderer if I hadn't run. Let's get out of here. I want to show you what I found out."

Back at the motel, Lin spread her printouts of Robert Randall across the desk. "I'm convinced that this Reverend Randall is actually Bobby Symms and that he was the subject of Delia's book, *Gory Alleluia*."

"That's a long way from finding Delia's killer, Lin." He reached into his briefcase. "Maybe it's time to show you these." He pulled out his computer-aged photographs. "Because he had such a prominent and identifiable cleft chin, I thought he might hide it with a beard, so I aged him with and without a beard. I didn't figure on him graying so early, so these show only slight traces of gray. But the likeness is pretty striking."

"Wow!" Lin said. "Striking is right! This is incredible. Now the children. What about the children?" She sucked in her breath as she stared at the enhancements Craig laid on the desk. She placed her finger on the man. "I knew it! That's Brad Benton, a co-worker—the one whose trophy replaced mine."

Craig hit the desk with his fist. "He must have known that his father was the book subject. He was probably still angry with you about Delia switching editors too. He must've seen a way to keep his secret and to set you up at the same time."

Lin said. "I imagine that poor Dottie surprised him, and he must've killed her too."

"No, she really was on a motor trip, but she's back. Pretty devastated too," Craig told her. "The computers weren't stolen at all. They were both in for repair, she said. One got a virus and the other caught it."

"Our trophies are identical except for the year and, of course, our names on the bottoms. Using gloves or a handkerchief so as not to add his fingerprints to mine, he must've taken my trophy and replaced it with his so that I wouldn't notice. I have no idea how long it was replaced."

"That makes it premeditated," Craig said, "but it is all circumstantial. It's not enough for a conviction, not even if we get a court order and have both Randall and Benton matched through DNA. Having a murdering father doesn't automatically make him a murderer too." He hugged Lin close to him and with his finger tilted her chin up so that she was facing him. "I think I can convince Trey to bring him in for questioning. Maybe we'll get lucky and he'll confess. Meanwhile, *querida*, if he realizes that you know what Delia knew, then you are in danger."

Lin wrapped her arms around his waist and enjoyed the tender moment. *Querida*. There was that word again.

"The difference is I know who he is, *mi tesoro*, my treasure. I can prepare." Her eyes fell on the girl's photo. She looked a lot like her father and Brad, right down to the cleft chin. How pitiful. She had both a father and a brother who were cold-blooded murderers. It is a blessing that she was adopted out with a brand-new identity. With any luck, she would never find out.

"We have an early flight back to New York so I'll meet you in the lobby at 6:30," Craig said. "I want you to get a good night's sleep. Doctor's orders. If you need me, I'm only four doors down. Call." He jotted down the number.

Lin licked her lips and titled her head expectantly. He kissed her on the forehead. "Lock up, *querida*."

She shut the door behind him, slid the lock into place, then tapped her forehead against the door a couple of times in frustration. A platonic kiss on the forehead after that passionate exchange in the car? *¡Ay chihuahua! He keeps me so off balance!*

Lin sighed in resignation. Craig was right to leave it at that, of course. Any more could have led to something extremely foolish and regrettable and very premature. She desperately needed to get her life straightened out. She didn't need to complicate it with an important relationship. And this had that potential, despite her self-doubts. Darn him, anyway! Why did he always have to be so right? *Tomorrow I'll be home. I will hug my dear little Jeffrey, and I'll give my findings to Lieutenant Trey. But what if it isn't enough to convince him to lock up Brad?*

Lin's body shivered. *Fox ran over your grave, niña.* She could be the next target.

CHAPTER 15

Lin slept soundly for the first time since Delia's murder, but she was showered, dressed, and packed by 5:30. When she was checking out, Craig arrived and signed out also. He slung her canvas bag over one shoulder and wrapped the other arm around Lin. "Ready to face the music, dear heart?"

Lin laughed. "As long as it isn't a harmonica in the next cell playing 'Nobody Knows the Trouble I've Seen.'" She felt such peace. Was it because she was going home or because of Craig, she wondered. She decided it was a little of both.

"Breakfast on the plane," Craig said as he started the car.

"I am beginning to think all you think about is food!" she said.

"Not all, *querida*, not all." He leaned over and gave her a lingering kiss before he put the car into drive.

Lin tried to think of something—anything—except how fast her head was spinning. She cleared her throat. "You roll your *r*'s like a true *tejano*," she said.

He pulled from the parking lot. "Is that all you are thinking?"

She smiled wryly. "Not all, *querido*, not nearly all."

At the airport, Craig turned in the car. Since neither of them had more than a single piece of carry-on luggage, they checked straight through. Lin was a bit startled to be seated in the first-class cabin. "Another of your tricks to dazzle me? I was rather hoping to see those 50 push-ups," she teased.

Soon after takeoff, the attendant brought orange juice, coffee, eggs Benedict, and fruit. "This is my first time on this side of the aisle curtain," she confessed. "I always had a sneaking suspicion that they were getting something better than scrambled eggs and cold rolls!"

Craig laughed. "Lin, you are such an intriguing combination of contrasts. I never know whether to expect the New York sophisticate or the little Texas girl. You make life very interesting."

Lin put down her fork and turned in her seat to face Craig. "Are you sure that Trey isn't going to arrest me for running off like that?" she asked.

Craig squeezed her hand. "If he does, I promise to bring you a giant cake with a saw in it." He frowned. "Trust me, Lin. Everything is okay."

Lin stirred her coffee. "I do; I mean, I try to. It's just so hard to trust in someone other than myself. I don't want to be hurt anymore."

"Mrs. Hill told me the circumstances. I understand. In my business, I've learned patience." He grinned. "You'll come around, *mi amor*. You'll see."

The attendant cleared the trays, and Lin snuggled against Craig's shoulder, dozing until the grind of the landing gears awoke her.

As they deplaned, Craig said, "I hate to tell you this, but I was in such a hurry that I didn't arrange for a car. I rode my motor to the airport. Are you game?"

"*¡Vámonos!* Let's go!" Lin said.

Craig grabbed her hand and the two of them dashed toward the exit. "That's my girl!" Craig said, laughing.

In the parking lot Craig handed her a helmet and strapped on his own. She straddled the seat behind him and wrapped her arms around his waist, shrieking joyfully as Craig throttled up. She couldn't help but laugh. If Papa could see her now, what would he think? His little girl, riding on *el diablo* with wheels.

At the duplex, Craig hung back until Lin had been properly hugged and greeted by the Hills. Mrs. Hill motioned for him to join them. "You should have seen Jeffrey when I told him that you two were on your way back here. I think even Sweetpea seemed to sense a good thing happening."

"I don't think I'm ready for a Sweetpea greeting," Lin said. "But I will stop by the school and reassure Jeffrey. I am so sorry for all the trouble, Mom, Dad. It was a foolish thing to do."

Craig placed his hands on Lin's shoulders and spun her to face him. "I know you have catching up to do, *querida*, so I'll head back and turn over our findings to Trey. I hope you won't even consider going in to work until Trey picks up Brad."

"I'll call first to be sure, I promise. And Craig—"

"Anytime, *mi amor*." He kissed her tenderly before roaring off on his Harley.

Lin stood watching until he had disappeared from sight. "You are so right, Mom. He is such a keeper!" She sucked in her breath and let it out slowly. The taste of his lips lingered on hers.

"I see that my Beetle is parked in front. How did it get here?" Lin asked.

"We knew you'd need it when you returned, so we drove to Indeco and retrieved it for you," Mr. Hill answered.

"Thanks, Dad. I'm going to run and see Jeffrey now. Then I think I'll take a drive out and see if I can find Dottie. She's got to know something about that manuscript. Maybe I'll take Sweetpea with me. He could use a good romp."

At the elementary school, Lin took Jeffrey out of class. When they were out of sight of his schoolmates, the two of them hugged. "Mom, I'm so glad to see you. Are you home for good?"

"Yes, Jeffrey. What did Grandma tell you about my trip?"

"She said you were in—investing, no—"

"Investigating?" Lin offered.

"Yeah, that's it. Investigating something real important. And Dr. Craig said that he would take good care of you, because he cared so much for us." Jeffrey grinned. "I like him a whole lot."

"So do I, Jeffrey. He said that? That he cared for *us*?"

"Uh-huh."

Lin said, "Time to get back to class. I'll see you at home, sweetheart." She walked him back to class.

Back home when Lin opened her door, Sweetpea made a wild, loving leap, landing with his front paws on Lin. She very nearly tumbled out the door from his weight. Rouster, sitting on his favorite spot on the back of the sofa, spat angrily and stalked into the kitchen.

"Okay, bad cat, for that you can be alone. Come on, Sweetpea. We're going back to your old haunts awhile. Maybe you'd like a good romp in the woods while I'm talking with Dottie."

When she arrived at the big double gates to Delia's estate, they were open and the crime tape was gone. A new white Corvette was parked next to Delia's car. "Wow, Sweetpea. Delia must have paid her secretary well, huh?"

Sweetpea leaped from the car. He circled the Corvette, sniffing and growling deep in his throat.

"Silly animal," Lin scolded. "It's just a car. A nice one, but still just a car." She walked around to the back with Sweetpea following. "Hello!" she called. "Dottie!" Lin slid the patio door open a crack. "Hello!"

Dottie was rummaging through the tapes on the bookshelves and seemed visibly shaken at Lin's appearance.

"Oh, I'm sorry to have startled you, Dottie. I—"

Sweetpea curled his lip in a snarl that showed his rows of bone-crushing teeth. A low guttural growl grew into loud snapping barks. He would have lunged at Dottie if Lin had not grabbed his collar. She used all her strength to hold him back, yelling, "Down! No!"

Dottie seemed frozen in place. Her face was etched with terror.

Lin squeezed through the opening into the room, leaving Sweetpea pawing at the glass door and barking furiously. "I'm so sorry, Dottie. I don't know what got into him. He's been an absolute lamb. Maybe he still senses this room and all that went on here. Dogs are extra sensitive, I'm told."

Dottie pushed her thick glasses back up on her nose. "I—I'm not much fond of animals. They don't like me; I think they know I'm scared of them."

"It must've been hard working for Delia then, with Sweetpea roaming about."

"Yes, ma'am. Uh, if you don't mind, I'm straightening things up."

Lin looked about her. It looked worse now than when she first saw the crime scene. "Dottie, I feel awkward asking this, but Delia's manuscript was already due, and I was hoping that you had the disk for me."

"No! That is, no, ma'am. I don't have any disk."

Lin walked into the office. "The computer is back. It wasn't here last time I looked."

Dottie stood between Lin and the computer. "You were here? Recently?"

"Yes, and both computers were gone. See if the manuscript is in the computer memory, Dottie. You did prepare it, didn't you?"

"Y—that is no, ma'am. Maybe she typed it herself."

Lin laughed. "That doesn't sound like Delia, does it? Why would she hire you if she was going to type it herself?"

"No, I remember. I typed it. But the computer files were corrupted. It ate all the files. They couldn't be retrieved." Dottie's hands flew to her glasses, then back to her side. She seemed agitated.

Lin stepped closer to Dottie. "Who was it about, Dottie?"

"I—I don't remember. I don't pay attention. I just let my fingers do the typing. I don't know."

"Wasn't it about Bobby Symms, also known as Reverend Robert Randall? Does that jog your memory, Dottie?"

Dottie whimpered.

Sweetpea's barking was louder. He rattled the door harder now.

"Delia found out about Bobby Symms, didn't she? She found out that his son was no other than Brad Benton. That must have been terribly upsetting since Brad got you this job. He was something of a mentor, wasn't he?"

Dottie sniffled, "Noooooooo. Doooon't. Please doooon't!"

"You don't have to be frightened, Dottie. A criminal always leaves something behind, always a clue. And you don't have to be afraid. He tried to pin it on me, but he couldn't hide his crime."

Sweetpea's howls were ear-shattering. The door thudded, as if he were throwing his huge body against it. Tears splashed down Dottie's face. She seemed near hysteria. She sidestepped slowly to the far side of the room. Lin saw the computer clearly for the first time. It had one of those tape drives, like the one at the library. "That's what he was looking for, what he tried to make Delia tell. A backup tape! The whole manuscript is on a tape, and she hid it. At your house? Think, Dottie. Did she give you a tape to keep?"

"No! Go away! Please!" Dottie screamed.

Lin moved closer to her. "It's all right, Dottie. You don't have to be afraid. Brad is being arrested even as we speak."

"No! Not Brad! Not—not Brad." Dottie took her glasses off and wiped her eyes.

For the first time, Lin saw Dottie without her thick, heavily framed glasses. She looked so different, so familiar, and yet . . . For the first time she noticed a faint perpendicular line on Dottie's chin, the remnants of plastic surgery, perhaps correcting a cleft chin. "*Dios mio*," she breathed. "You are the daughter. You are Bobby Symms's daughter! It was you, not Brad, who murdered Delia!"

Dottie made an almost animal sound as she dove at Lin, grabbing her by the throat. The two of them tumbled to the floor, rolling side to side with Lin flailing at Dottie, trying to break her grip. Lin gasped for her breath. She could feel herself growing faint. With one last effort, she clapped her open hands against Dottie's ears. Dottie shrieked and let go long enough for Lin to gulp in a deep breath. The two struggled to their feet.

Using the side of her foot, Lin kicked Dottie's knee joint, breaking her balance so that she crumpled to the floor. There was a crash as the patio door gave way beneath Sweetpea's thrusts, and he was suddenly on top of Dottie, snapping at her.

Dottie rolled into a fetal position sobbing violently. Sweetpea lay across her, pinning her down. His huge mouth spread in a tongue-lolling grin.

"Good dog, Sweetpea," Lin said, coughing and gasping for her breath. She reached for the phone to dial for help when she heard voices.

It was Trey, Craig, and Brad. Craig grabbed Lin by the shoulders. "Are you all right? Lin, let me look at you." He turned her head side to side, inspecting the welts on her neck. "Thank God."

"I—I was just about to call you. How did you know?" She pulled Sweetpea off Dottie so that Trey could lift her to her feet.

"When Brad told us how his trophy came to be on your desk, it all fell into place—more or less, with the help of your discoveries," Trey said. "He knew his sister had a problem about, uh, taking things that didn't belong to her. He tried to cover for her."

"I thought I could replace your trophy with mine until I could get yours back from her," Brad said. "I never meant any harm to come to you. She's my sister, though. I had to protect her. You understand?" He turned to his sister. "Why, Dottie? I can't help you this time."

Dottie said, "Delia was going to tell everything. I—I couldn't let her do that. I destroyed the computer files. But I couldn't find the tape, and she wouldn't tell me where it was. She told me she would, so I untied her, but she lied."

"Why Lin's trophy, Dottie?" Brad asked.

"She saw the trophy sticking out of my purse and recognized it. It's pretty; I liked to have it with me. I couldn't let her fire me. I just hit her, and I hit her again."

Trey handcuffed Dottie and led her out to the patrol car. Brad hesitated. "I really am sorry, Lin. Dottie is all the family I have, you know." He followed Trey out.

Lin let herself be swept into Craig's arms. "I was so wrong about Brad, poor guy. I thought I was being so clever."

"You said all along that when you knew the subject of *Gory Alleluia* you'd know the murderer; you were half right. And you darn near got yourself killed for it."

Lin laughed. "Not with Superdog here. And you laughed when I said he was a witness! He knew!" She reached down to pat Sweetpea on the head. "Come on, brave one, I guess that lets you out of the doghouse for all the trouble you've caused."

She shrieked. "That's it! D's hows. Dog's house! Delia knew that Dottie wouldn't go around Sweetpea, so she hid the tape in the doghouse!" She grabbed Craig's hand and tugged him out to the huge doghouse in the back property. Lin dropped to her knees. She felt around inside the door. "Yes!" She emerged triumphantly with a cassette cartridge.

*   *   *

Over the next few weeks, as Lin edited Delia's manuscript, she learned that Randall had been scamming his growing flock of followers for millions of dollars. When Delia found that his credentials were phony, she somehow connected him to Bobby Symms. How, Lin still couldn't figure out. Indeco rushed the book into publication. It was perfect timing; the evening before the release date, TV news carried a story about the capture and return to Louisville of Bobby Symms, aka Reverend Robert Randall. The announcer said that the case had been broken by retired detective Joseph Leopold, acting on a tip.

Lin joined Craig and Jeffrey, her two favorite fellows, on the front steps of the duplex to watch the sun set over the park trees across the way. "You know, the irony of all this is that Delia dealt only with Randall and his dual identity; there was no mention of Brad or Dottie. She may not have known that she was dictating her story to one of the children until it was too late. The murder was all for nothing."

"Saving the family reputation wasn't Dottie's motive, Lin. She knew about her father even before Delia's manuscript," Craig said. "She was blackmailing him. If the story came out, she'd no longer have anything on him. Her money supply would dry up. Not even Brad knew that Symms was their birth father."

As they watched, the sky turned amber, then darkened to indigo. "The evening star, *niño*; make a wish," Lin told Jeffrey.

"I already did, Mom. You make one too."

Lin wrapped one arm around Jeffrey and one around Craig. "Ummmm," she said, *"mi vida y mi hijo*, love of my life and my son. There is nothing left to wish for. It doesn't get better than this."

Craig smiled at her. "Oh, yes, *querida*, it does. Trust me."